"*I personally know how difficult men and their families. I have r. now and I personally know that he has done a lot of good for a lot of young men and their families. His book, The Storm will only compound the good that he does for families and their young struggling men.*"

— Tebucky Jones, New England Patriots Super Bowl Champion

"*Daniel Blanchard's parenting book The Storm is a book I feel very lucky to have had the opportunity to read. Reading this book feels like sitting down with a good friend, someone who really cares about you and wants to share secrets with you to inspire, uplift, and challenge you to live a truly meaningful life. The Storm has many valuable, commonsense lessons that can help anyone of us live a life full of promise, a life that we can truly be proud of. Sometimes even with the best of intentions, we feel stuck, unable and unsure how we can achieve our goals. The Storm will give you that extra nudge to go after your dreams, stop holding on to a past that may be holding you back, believe in yourself, and give you the resolve once and for all to take control of your life.*"

"*Anyone who has ever said or thought, 'I wish I knew then I what I know now' needs to get a copy of The Storm, read it, and then pass it on to a loved one.*"

— Princess Betsey Katiti

"*Dan Blanchard is a hero in our family. He was a great role model and a source of inspiration for my boys when they were in high school. He helped them grow up to be good men and now he is sharing his heart-touching story, The Storm, which will do the same for you, your sons, and your family!*"

— Paula Mele, Mrs. International CT

Cover Illustrator: Emily Mann
Editor: Valerie Utton
Interior Design: 1106 Design
Published by:
Teen Leadership Publishing
www.GranddaddysSecrets.com

Print: 978-0-9862398-2-3

eBook: 978-0-9862398-1-6

Printed in the United States of America

THE STORM

THE STORM

HOW YOUNG MEN
BECOME GOOD MEN

DAN BLANCHARD

Book Series Page of Dan Blanchard

Granddaddy's Secrets Book Series

Granddaddy's Secrets for Educators Book Series

Authors Should Speak Book Series

Granddaddy's Secrets for Sports Lovers Book Series

Granddaddy's Secrets for Parents Book Series

Granddaddy's Secrets for Self-Starters Book Series

Granddaddy's Secrets for Frustration Beaters Book Series

Granddaddy's Secrets for Overachievers Book Series

Granddaddy's Secrets for Authorpreneurs Book Series

*Please follow Dan on Amazon:

http://www.amazon.com/-/e/B00KEO611E

ACKNOWLEDGEMENTS

A special thanks to my beautiful wife Jennifer and our five precious children: Kalaiya, Dakota, Savanna, Aliya, and Seanna. They were all extremely patient with the many hours it took to create this book.

A special thanks to my editor, Valerie Utton, who always has great advice and plenty of thought-provoking questions to ask.

Thank you to all the students I've had the pleasure of meeting over the years. You inspired me to write this book.

Further gratitude goes to our free public libraries. Even after all these years, I continue to learn from the books I find there.

Lastly, thank you to all the people, family, and friends who have inspired and supported me on this journey.

Sincerely,
Daniel R. Blanchard

TABLE OF CONTENTS

*"Too many people waste their lives waiting
for their lucky break.*

*What they fail to realize is that luck isn't something
you can wait for."* —Daniel Blanchard

"Luck is when preparation meets opportunity." —Seneca

FOREWORD

—by Colleen Ferrary

Dan Blanchard's mother left this world too soon from too hard of a life. She raised seven kids on her own while being married to an emotionally and physically abusive alcoholic husband. Unfortunately, she didn't get to see that her son Dan had overcome the odds (and his anger towards his father) and had grown up to become a good man and a great father himself. This Father of five has gone on to receive numerous degrees, become a teacher, a Junior Olympic Wrestling coach and sought after speaker.

Although I didn't work the graveyard shift and raise 7 children like Dan's mom, as a single mom I personally know how hard it is to work and raise a family. But the good thing is, that it can be done, and it can be done successfully. Through working really hard - like Dan's mom - I managed to become successful as the President and founder of Small Business USA LLC and Co-Founder and Managing Partner of Generating Winners LLC while also successfully raising a child of my own in a loving and supportive home.

I met Dan a few years ago after being moved by one of his inspiring speeches at The Hartford-Springfield Speakers Network and eventually recruited him to be on the Board of Generating Winners. Throughout the time I have known Dan, I have come to see that he is an amazingly high-energy dynamic type man. He works harder than anyone I know inspiring others. He shares his wealth of knowledge to support his life's mission of helping teens live a better life.

Dan shows us how good boys can become good men through introducing parents and their sons to a very successful role model - Granddaddy. Granddaddy is one of the main characters of Dan's new book, *The Storm*. This is the first book in *Granddaddy's Secrets* book series. *The Storm* is a teen leadership book of a boy coming into his own presented as a parable that gently walks teens and their guardians through a story of sage advice that consists of the marshmallow test, planning ahead, the power of forgiving, knowing thyself, calling people by their names and kaizen, as well as much, much more. Dan is a master at gently encouraging people to think about themselves and their own self-development in a non-threatening and judgement-free manner.

I'm often told that my forte as a mom, author and business owner is that I have consistently been able to deliver the gift of inspiration combined with fierce strategy to help people overcome challenges in their quest to live a rich and fulfilling life. I would argue that Dan and his Granddaddy from *The Storm* are doing the same thing. Dan is a living example of someone with a fiercely competitive spirit for success and with a kind heart that is just as big. Most people don't realize Dan's stories hale from experience. Dan has overcome all sorts of obstacles from almost being aborted, to deaf and mute, to fighting for his life with meningitis, and fighting for survival in the tough streets of the north end of Hartford. He's overcome all these challenges while coming from a poverty stricken and abusive home. Overcoming all of these obstacles has molded Dan into the type of good man that is probably the only type of man that could have created the wise, empathetic, and resilient Granddaddy character of *The Storm* and *The Granddaddy's Secrets* book series.

Parents, you and your sons are going to love this book. You'll surely bond with Granddaddy while learning ways of thinking that foster self-improvement and great behaviors. Through Granddaddy's insights on how to be the best possible person that one can be, he and Dan will help turn good boys into the good men that we so desperately need today during these times of turbulence, violence and lack of leadership.

Enjoy the story! I know I did!

THE SMELL OF RAIN

"Out of difficulties grow miracles." —Jean De La Bruyere

"Dakota, I smell the coming of rain," Granddaddy said as we walked through the park on this cool, breezy fall day.

I gave him a sideways look, thinking how weird his statement was and couldn't help but notice Granddaddy was still in pretty good shape for an old guy. I haven't seen him a lot over the years, but he hasn't changed much. His body is still lean and muscular. He still cuts his hair the same way—military style.

I don't know how old he is, but I'm certain he's a lot older than he looks. The only thing that's really changed over the years is that his hair has turned grey. It looks good though; kind of majestic even. He definitely looks like the kind of guy who's been around and just knows stuff.

As I was studying him, I realized that in some ways his physique is kind of like mine—a much older version, of course. He must have read my mind because he looked at me like he was sizing me up too.

"You've been working out, Dakota... A lot by the looks of it," he said.

"Yup." I flexed a bicep to show off a little.

"You know, you remind me a little bit of myself when I was your age," he said with a nod of approval. "Of course you are your own man. You aren't me. You aren't your father, either. You're just you. Dakota. So... are you wondering why I chose the park for us to spend this special day together?"

"Sure."

"Because this is the perfect place for me to share some very important lessons with you today."

"Lessons? Lessons for what?" I asked.

"You'll see," he said. "But once you learn these lessons, you'll have a deeper understanding of how to make your way in this world. You'll be better prepared to grow into someone people will respect and look up to. You won't have to settle for anything, either. You'll be able to choose work you love, but also work that has purpose and meaning. You'll be in a position to be a leader too. People will respect you as a leader, and as a leader, in one way or another, you'll be well compensated for your contributions to making this world a better place for yourself and everyone else you come in contact with."

"That sounds good," I said thoughtfully. A leader? I hadn't really thought of myself as a leader, but I liked the sound of it. I liked the thought of being able to make decisions instead of being told what to do.

Granddaddy continued, "The first of these very important lessons is represented by this walk in the park. The lesson is that the simple things in life really can be some of the best things in life. Always make time in your busy life to enjoy them. Take a relaxing walk in the park. Take time to appreciate a sunrise or a sunset. Take a moment to admire a bird in flight. Remember and cherish your first kiss with your girlfriend."

He stopped walking and looked straight at me.

"Don't let your life get so complicated that you end up negotiating away your values and not living up to your highest potential. Never forget the miracle you truly are, or all the miracles you're surrounded by every day. When you take the time to look at the world and begin to see all the possibilities around you, you'll always be able to find the strength to do what's right." He smiled and then looked up at the sky.

"Yup. Definitely a storm on the way."

I looked up at the sky and then at him, but he'd started walking again. My gut was telling me there was some truth to what he was saying, but I didn't really see him often enough to know if I could trust everything he said. Maybe he was just a cool older guy who told good stories.

He had an aura of authority, though, and talked with the deliberate wisdom of an old soldier. I knew he'd seen a lot as a World War II fighter pilot, but I wasn't convinced he could smell the "coming of rain." I sniffed the air, but I couldn't smell anything. I couldn't see any shelter to run to even if it did start to rain. He must have been reading my mind.

"It'll be okay. I've weathered many storms in my life much worse than the one headed our way," he said clapping a hand on my shoulder. "I know you're only 16 years old Dakota, but I have the feeling you might have already weathered a few storms worse than the one headed this way too."

At first, I thought he was talking about the rain, but Granddaddy had a way of talking about things that made a person think. It was one of the things I liked about him.

Granddaddy continued walking.

"As a matter of fact, as unusual as it may sound, I love rain storms now. Maybe you will too someday. They remind me of the awesome power of my Creator. Rain doesn't discriminate. If we get caught in the rain, it will soak us without a care for who we are or where we came from. It doesn't matter how soaked we get, either. The enduring power of the sun will indiscriminately dry all of us off.

"Getting caught in the rain reminds me of how strong and how weak we can be at the exact same time. The rain and the sun are two more of life's miracles working together to remind us of life's cycles. Sort of like the movie *The Lion King* and the circle of life it described. Of course, the big difference between the real thing and the movie is that the movie is the same every time you watch it. The rain, the sun, our lives... well... they're all a little bit more unpredictable. When you pay attention, though, it gets easier to figure out what's important and what's trivial. If things seem overwhelming, just look up at the sky and suddenly your problems will seem small alongside all the majesty and wonder going on up there."

I looked up at the sky again, trying to figure out what Granddaddy was saying without having to ask him to explain it. His words made me think about thunderstorms and maybe even about other kinds of storms I'd gone through over the years. I remember what they'd felt like, and I didn't like thinking about those times any more than I liked the thought of getting caught in the rain today. What did he know about me? Did he know about my past? How could he? He wasn't around enough to know that much, but he was right about one thing: I did have a tough life.

School wasn't easy for me. Home wasn't much better. It was always loud, chaotic, and stressful, just like it was for everyone else who lived in my neighborhood. At least I'd learned a few things to make it easier to deal with. And what could I do about it anyway? That was the way life was for us. And even though my life wasn't perfect, I still had a better life than a lot of other people. At least I had my sports and a great girlfriend.

My girlfriend is the best thing in my life. She's tall, very athletic, and beautiful. She has big, beautiful brown eyes and long, flowing hair that's brown with blond highlights. Sometimes she reminds me of one of those music divas—minus the attitude. She's awesome at basketball and track and is a great person with a heart of gold. She's perfect, except for the fact that she's always losing her keys.

I think it's so cute when she loses them. I try not to laugh while she fumbles through her purse trying to find them. After a few failed attempts, she gets frustrated, sighs, and then tips her purse upside down, spilling the contents onto the table. Then presto, like magic, the keys are there, sitting on top of the rubble she calls "all her stuff."

I know how fortunate I am to have someone like her in my life because most of my friends aren't as lucky. They don't have someone solid in their life; someone they can count on and hold on to when times are tough. It probably feels to them like the sun doesn't shine much in their world. For them, it's dark skies and storm clouds most of the time. My girlfriend is like the sun. I just feel better when she's around.

It's tough when you feel like there's no one around who cares. I guess that might be one of the reasons so many of my old friends have turned away from school, sports, and even the law. They don't feel like there's anybody who really cares about them. Instead, they turn to gangs and end up a part of all the drugs, crime, and fighting that comes along with them.

It doesn't seem that long ago that we used to laugh and play in the streets and didn't have to worry about looking over our shoulder all the time. We played sports and pretended we were superstars hitting home runs, scoring touchdowns, or sinking the winning basket.

I miss those days sometimes. We used to have such a great time. We had our sports and our friendships, but time kept moving and we started getting caught up in what was going on around us. Before too long, we were fighting in the streets too. After a while, we turned to different things.

I stuck with sports and joined teams. I learned it took discipline to get better and I liked it. I liked the routine. I learned about persistence, but my old friends didn't see the value of organized sports. To them, it looked like too much work and too much being bossed around. For me, it was an outlet. I got to channel the same frustration, anger, and aggression we all felt into something a whole other group of people cheered for.

I like how physically demanding the sports I play are. I get a kick out of the fact that it's legal to hit the enemy as hard as I can on the football field without worrying about being arrested for it. I find it amazing that people praise me and admire me for brawling on the wrestling mat in front of stands full of bystanders instead of suspending me. Even the principal watches and then congratulates me after I've skillfully nailed my opponent to the ground.

With sports, I get to focus all my intensity into becoming a force to be reckoned with in both wrestling and football. Turning to sports made it easier for me to walk away from fighting in the streets.

Now I put my energy to good use by putting up a good fight in competitive sports. I know I'm only 16 years old, but I'm pretty lucky to have already figured out other ways to channel my anger. I use it to punish the weights in the weight room with a ferocity rarely seen in guys my age. I've grown muscle and developed incredible strength for my age too. Being so strong has also enabled me to keep up with the older varsity guys in both football and wrestling.

I know playing sports has helped keep me out of trouble with the police too. In my neighborhood, probably a lot of neighborhoods, you don't always have to be committing a crime to get the police to pay attention to you. They still might look at me now, but it's different.

Playing sports has created this weird phenomenon in my life. In general, people look at me differently. They don't look at me like I'm a thug or another "reject" from the streets. They don't talk about me as just another one of those kids who grew up in a "dysfunctional" family. Instead, people respect me.

Strangers say hi to me everywhere I go. They tell me they saw me play or wrestle or that they'd read in the newspaper about what I did. People are always congratulating me now. Once a kid even asked me for my autograph! It blows my mind that I get all this positive attention for putting up a good fight in sports rather than on the streets! Sometimes it's a little strange too because it feels like people are watching me and waiting to see what I'll do next. But maybe that's what people do anyway. They just kind of watch each other to see who's going to do something worth watching.

How strange life is! Sometimes my thoughts wander, and I start thinking really deep about the things going on around me, or about things I read in school, and then it's like I become the watcher. Sometimes I get really deep into my thoughts and start making weird paradoxical connections, like seeing the adults at school telling kids not to be angry and not to fight, but then turning around and praising me for putting up a good fight in sports.

I also think that in a bizarre way, my experience from the streets and the anger I felt as a result of some of the things I've had to deal with have been beneficial to me. Would I have made the varsity wrestling team as a freshman without any formal training if I hadn't started on the streets?

I don't know. I know there's a big difference between a 14-year-old and an 18-year-old. Fourteen-year-olds are usually significantly over-matched and can't compete against 18-year-olds.

Fourteen-year-olds with no formal training just don't make varsity teams. But I did! Some people say I'm a natural, and maybe they're right, but I want to believe there's more to it than that. I mean... I'm the one who did it, right?

Okay, I might have gotten a head start with wrestling from fighting when I was younger. But then I learned about gladiators, and I wondered if maybe they grew up dealing with some of the same stuff. Did Roman adults go around telling Rome's gladiators not to be angry or fight in the streets when they were growing up? Some of those ancient gladiators made it all the way to the Roman Coliseum!

I know we need order in this world, but I think it's a little bit ironic. When we're kids, they tell us not to fight, but we have famous warriors in our history books and famous prize fighters on TV. They tell us not to do it, but the better we are at it, the more handsomely paid and praised we are for it.

Sometimes it feels like there's a lot of distance between the streets and the arena. There wasn't really any "glory of the battle" when I was fighting—just survival. I didn't want to continue with the chaos of that path even though a lot of my old friends are still there. My decision to focus on sports has been much more productive than fighting in the streets and it keeps me out of trouble.

I just wish my old friends had chosen sports over the streets too!

THE STORM

"By the time a man realizes that maybe his father was right, he usually has a son who thinks he's wrong."
—Charles Wadsworth

I thought I felt a drop of rain splat on the rim of my ball cap and stuck my hand out, palm up, to see if it was starting to rain. It wasn't. I was glad because I was feeling pretty fortunate to be spending time with my Granddaddy today. It's November 30th and it's my birthday. It's the greatest day for a birthday as far as I'm concerned because it lands right between the end of the fall sports season and the beginning of the winter sports season—perfect timing.

To tell the truth, I'm surprised he came around today. I haven't seen him in a long time, and he didn't come by for my birthday last year. When my mom told me he was coming by today and wanted to talk to me, I was a little nervous. I thought maybe he was going to tell me he was dying or something crazy like that, but I heard him say to my mom, "Don't you worry about me. I've got way too many things to do and dyin' isn't on the list."

I guess we have that in common too. Like him, I have a very busy life. There's school, sports, and my morning paper route. I also have my part-time job at the gas station. I work there after practice on school nights and then the entire day on

Sunday. Saturday is always game day, so I'm busy pretty much every minute of every day.

Some days I wish I had a few more hours to work with so it would be easier to get things done—like homework. There are definitely times when I end up winging it or not doing it at all. I know that's not good, but I seem to get by and somehow manage to pass my classes. In the end, I guess that's all that really matters, right?

Granddaddy hasn't said much yet, but he's already got me thinking. I don't think he wants to talk to me because he's dying, either. He looks healthy. I think he wants to talk to me because he has something he wants me to hear. Weird, but he's a cool guy, and I want to hear what he has to say.

Today's the perfect day because it's between seasons so I don't have practice or a game, and I don't have to be at work until much later. I wonder if he knew that before today. It would be nice if he had. It would mean he really did make the trip just to talk to me. I know he didn't spend much time with Pops when Pops was a kid, but I don't feel sorry for Pops because he did the same thing to me. He could have been different with me and spent time with me, but he didn't.

Maybe it runs in the family. Pops spends the same amount of time with me that his dad spent with him. I'm too busy to spend a lot of time with anyone, except for my girlfriend, and I'm not around for her as much as she would like, either. Still, it got me thinking. If I have a son, will I end up doing the same thing to him?

From generation to generation, it looks like the cycle keeps repeating itself in my family. I wonder if it happened to Granddaddy too. It makes me think about my old friends. I don't know if I remember their dads being around much either. What if this doesn't just happen to people like me, or people in my neighborhood? What if it's happening to most people? What if it's the way it is in our society, and families aren't spending time together like they used to? Man, I'm just a regular philosopher today.

Isn't it weird how life works out sometimes, though; how the same things cycle around in different kinds of ways? The pattern continues with just enough variation to make it harder to see. Most of us never even notice it because we're stuck right in the middle of it. We're too busy thinking about how everything is affecting us, all wrapped and trapped inside an invisible cycle. Is that what Granddaddy meant when he was talking about the cycle of life and the coming storm?

I don't know what happened between Granddaddy and Pops. All I know is that Granddaddy doesn't come around. Pops is an angry guy in general, but he does seem to get a certain kind of angry when Granddaddy shows up.

My mom says Granddaddy was never around when Pops needed him. Instead he was always too busy trying to make money and succeed. Every time Granddaddy comes around, she tells me not to be like him. She says he neglected his kids in order to spend more time at the office, and that's why Pops is always angry. If Granddaddy had been there for him, then maybe Pops would have been more of a success and he wouldn't have any reason to drink.

I don't know, though. Pops hasn't been around for me, and I succeed once in a while. Maybe not all the time, but when I do, it's because I did something pretty good. Truth is, I don't much care what Pops thinks about what I do. Well, maybe that's not exactly true; I do care, I just don't let caring stop me from doing.

After I'd won my first wrestling match, I was so excited. As soon as I got home, I told Pops. No response. So I went to my bedroom and closed the door. I felt so stupid. Why did I think anything I did would impress him? My mom came into my room and told me that success comes from inside. That it's something you feel when you look at the results of your contribution. It doesn't come from other people, titles, or your reputation. You can have all those things without feeling like you've succeeded.

It made me feel a little better, but it also made me wonder if Pops thought of himself as a success. Probably not. If what Mom says is right about Pop's and Granddaddy's relationship, then it sounds like Pops is still rebelling against his father and using that as his excuse to drink too much and treat his family badly.

Mom says that a lot of people have the formula for success wrong. They chase the outer world rather than their inner world. What they need to do is to take the time to understand what Jesus was really saying when he told us the Kingdom of Heaven was within each of us. God bless Mom! She really is the rock and bread of this family!

But how crazy is it that after all this time Pops is still using Granddaddy as his excuse? Are adults really just big kids running around with the same emotions and feelings as kids my age? I might only be 16, but it seems to me that Pops is the pot calling the kettle black. If he was so upset by the way Granddaddy treated him, then why doesn't he make an effort to spend time with me?

I guess the big difference with the cycle this time around is that I'm fine with him not being around much. When he does come home, it's usually late and he's usually drunk. He's angry, mean, and abusive. He doesn't do it now, not since my big brother put a stop to it, but he used to come home and start beating on all of us... me, my brother, and my mother. I've never been able to figure out what we did to make him so angry. I've thought about it a lot, though.

The thing is, none of us had anything to do with the fact that Granddaddy wasn't there for him. None of us even existed when that happened. Maybe when he looks at me all he sees is the underachiever he is, and it's too painful for him. Maybe he hates me because I actually succeed at stuff and he hates that I can do things he didn't, or couldn't do. Is it possible he's jealous and was trying to beat the success right out of me? To tell you the truth, I don't know what he sees when he looks at me.

Pops wasn't home today when Granddaddy arrived and I'm glad he wasn't. I've never talked with Granddaddy about Pops and I don't want to. I'm just glad to spend time with him. It's nice to have someone talking to me instead of yelling at me. I like telling him about the things I've done. He nods like he knows what I'm talking about. Maybe I'm an overachiever like he is. I'd like to think I'm burning with desire not to be anything like Pops.

It makes me angry to think about this, but if Pops had been a real dad instead of an angry, frustrated man pretending to be my father, I believe my life would be better. At the very least, my stomach probably wouldn't freeze up every time I hear him come home at night wondering what kind of mood he's in. If he'd cared about me, he could have taught me what it means to be a good dad. Instead, he taught me how to be angry. I still get angry, but I know the difference between taking it out on a person and using it as fuel for a workout.

When I'm a dad I'm going to do a better job. I don't exactly know how to do it—it's not like Pops showed me what a good dad does. But I know I won't treat my kids the way Pops treats me. I'm going to be there for my kids. I will break this cycle! I will be the one who everyone in this future family tree looks up to as the one who changed it all, the hero!

I looked sideways at Granddaddy and could just barely hear him humming. I don't know if he was humming an actual song, but to me it was more evidence that he's nothing like Pops. I've never seen him angry and never heard him yell— not even at Pops. It makes me wonder if he ever gets angry.

If Granddaddy had been the kind of dad who hit, I think I'd know. I'm not the only guy with a dad who hits. I know a lot of guys who've been hit by their dads. It's not like they announce it, we all just kind of know. I guess that means their dads are angry too. Is that the reason so many of my old friends seem to be getting angrier as time goes by? Or is that the way it is in rough and tough neighborhoods and schools like mine?

I don't want to believe all this anger is normal, but it seems to be normal where 1 live. People are always yelling about something in my neighborhood. When I go to a friend's home there's usually someone yelling there too. My teachers and coaches are constantly yelling at the students and athletes. All I see around me is a very loud world full of chaos. I think it's normal because I'm used to it. I sure hope it isn't like this everywhere on the planet. It would suck to find out the whole world is like this.

But Granddaddy's not angry, and I know he grew up some-where around here. I wonder where he lives now. Maybe he lives in another part of the world the rest of us don't know about. If he does live in some special place, who else lives there and what kinds of things do they talk about? Can I go there or is it so secret it's closed off to people like me because of where we come from? What's the weather like there? Is it always sunny or do they have storms like the one Granddaddy can smell coming?

If there is a place like that, I hope Granddaddy tells me about it. Maybe he's trying to figure out if I'm good enough to move there. I want to be, but I don't know if I am. Or maybe this other place is some kind of crazy secret society or cult!

I don't know if there is such a place; there probably isn't. It's just It's just the philosopher part of me getting carried away and thinking all these crazy thoughts. What I can't figure out is if Granddaddy really did grow up in the same crazy, loud, chaotic world I'm living in. According to my mom, he did. If he did, then how did he escape?

I know he fought Hitler in World War II. Maybe he learned something from that, but he doesn't talk about it and I don't ask.

If he was around more I might, but he isn't. Instead, I listen to him hoping he'll tell me more stories about his life.

There are a lot of things I like about him. He's always so peaceful for one. It's like he likes himself and because he does, it makes it easy for people to like him right back.

He's confident too. He doesn't act like he knows every-thing; he acts like he's happy knowing what he knows. He al-ways seems to have someplace to go, but he's not nervous about getting there either. When he's ready to leave, he just looks at his watch and says,

"Would you look at the time. Gotta hit the road."

SKATE TO WHERE THE PUCK IS GOING!

<hr/>

"Efforts and courage are not enough without purpose and direction." —John F. Kennedy

"Let's go this way, Dakota," Granddaddy said, pointing to the right. "If I remember correctly, there's a pavilion with a red picnic table on the other side of those big pine trees."

I thought I knew this park by heart, but I couldn't remember ever seeing a pavilion with a picnic table.

"We can sit and let the pavilion shelter us from the storm."

"Can you really smell the rain coming?" I asked.

"I sure can," he replied with a big smile and then sniffed at the air. "It's even stronger now. It's going to start raining any time now." I gave him a sideways look.

"Don't look so doubtful. Being able to smell a storm brewing is an easy skill to develop. All you have to do is start paying attention to what the air smells like. Take a deep breath when you go outside. After a while you'll be able to tell when it's going to rain or snow or be sunny just by the smell of the air. Can you do that?"

I nodded my head and took a deep breath. I still couldn't smell anything, but I was willing to give it a try.

Granddaddy smiled. "Good. Glad we got that out of the way because I have a lot more secrets I want to share with you today."

He was going to share secrets with me? Secrets? Actual secrets? My heart quickened.

"Well, a lot of people think of them as secrets simply because they've never heard them before. When we started walking, I didn't use the word secrets, though; I used the word lessons. I used that word first because I wanted to see if you'd be interested in hearing what I had to say."

"I'm in. I want to hear whatever you have to say. Did you think I wouldn't listen because you used the word lesson?"

Granddaddy shrugged. "Not exactly... I just know from experience that sometimes people are willing to hear what you have to say and sometimes they aren't. We all know what lessons are. Sometimes we learn them in school. Other times we learn them as a result of something we did. Did you ever burn your finger on a match?"

"Probably."

"Have you done it again?"

"That wouldn't be very smart... doing it twice."

"You're right. You learned your lesson the first time. The way I figure it, a lesson is something you can learn, but after you have a real life experience with applying a lesson, it turns into something more. I could just sit here and recite the lessons I'd like you to learn. But that's not what I have in mind. The secrets I want to share with you can be used to build a meaningful and successful life. For example, do you know what the great hockey player Wayne Gretzky said when he was asked what the secret to his success was?" "No," I answered.

He leaned closer and said, "He said he never skated to where the puck was, but rather to where the puck was going to be. He always planned ahead and that's what made him a success and a superstar."

"Hmm, I guess that makes sense," I replied.

"It does," Granddaddy said. "You must always plan ahead. It's a way of preparing for whatever happens next. Like right now. I planned ahead, and now when it starts raining we'll be dry instead of getting soaked."

"So coming here was part of a plan," I said.

"Well, I knew it was going to rain, and I knew I wanted to talk to you somewhere where there wouldn't be a lot of other people around. I remembered this place, so yes, I planned ahead."

I nodded and tried not to smile. How cool was it that he had taken the time just to talk to me?

"But there's another important thing about this plan I want you to be aware of. I didn't just plan to keep myself dry. I planned it so we would both be dry."

It was starting to rain now, and Granddaddy nodded his head thoughtfully. "The other thing that made Gretzky great was that his planning didn't create a level of success that only benefited him. His plan, and ultimately his success, had a huge impact on the whole team's success.

"When you make plans, you want to remember that a lot of the time your success has the power to influence the success of the people around you, whether it's as part of a team, at home, or out in your community. So when you decide which dreams you want to pursue and start planning for, make sure your vision includes success for the people around you too. It doesn't

25

matter whether we're talking about sports or life, either. Most people are too mentally lazy to think about anything beyond getting what they want, so they don't put any extra energy or thought into planning for anyone or anything beyond themselves. Instead, they nonchalantly wing it, hoping no one will notice, or that someone else will be there to pick up their slack. And then they brag about winging it like it's something to be proud of!"

Granddaddy shook his head. "You're already a good planner and you're only 16. That's good because as you get older you're going to see a lot of people who are still winging it... It's one thing to wing it when you haven't studied as hard as you should have for a test. It's another thing to wing it when you have a family that's relying on you."

I wondered if Granddaddy somehow knew I hadn't studied for my last test. I had definitely winged it. Still... I got a C+.

"When people don't take the time to make plans, they give up any control they might have over the results they're going to get. They have almost no chance of winning. Worse than that, they aren't likely to be in a position to help others. Do you know what a kayak looks like, Dakota?"

Granddaddy was talking like I think sometimes, moving from one thought to another without a pause in between, but I was determined to keep up with him.

"Sure. I know what a kayak is."

"It's like they've gotten into a kayak and started floating down a lazy river. It might be okay for a while, but as soon as it starts getting rough, or they want to stop or change direction, they can't because they didn't plan well enough to bring a paddle. Without a paddle, they're at the mercy of the river currents.

They might even start picking up speed or hit white-water rapids. They might be heading towards a damn or waterfall. Will they survive? Maybe, but if they'd planned on bringing a paddle, they would have been a lot better prepared and might have even enjoyed the challenges the river presented."

"You'd have to be pretty dumb to forget a paddle," I said.

"Well, what if they didn't know they needed a paddle?" Granddaddy asked and shook his head. "I know that sounds weird, but we're not really talking about a kayak. We're talking about people setting out to do something figuring they'll be able to wing it. If no one tells them they need a paddle, and they don't put enough thought or planning into it before they step into the kayak, how are they going to know they need one?" "That's crazy," I said.

"It is," he replied. "Eventually, these people realize the trouble they're in and either panic or shut down. Either way, they started out without the tools or knowledge they needed to keep themselves out of trouble. Even if they somehow manage to come through it okay, it's not like they can take credit for what they've done, because they didn't do anything. They can't feel like they've accomplished or achieved anything, either... because they haven't."

I stared at the rain drops starting to drip off the edge of the roof, thinking about how stupid it would be to get into a kayak without a paddle. Then I turned and smiled at him.

"I can honestly say that I don't think I've ever done anything that stupid."

He looked at me thoughtfully. "As far as I know, you haven't, but people don't plan to be dumb. They just end up doing dumb things when they don't plan. What if it was you in that kayak and it was a two-seater kayak and you had your five-year-old son in the front seat?"

I frowned. "I'd make sure I had a paddle and that he was wearing a life preserver."

"Exactly. But you're already a good planner. Too many people aren't, and when they aren't, it's the people who are counting on them who suffer the most. And I'm not going to lie to you. Some people wing it most of the time and do surprisingly well for a while. But that's an exception, not the rule. People who experience success without any planning or effort have no idea what to do when things stop going their way. They never had a plan A, which means they don't have a plan B. Planning your life gives you options.

"Gretzky's plan A was to skate to where the puck was going to be. We have to do the same thing. Figure out where we want to be and then make a plan to get there. If we don't, trust me, society will be right there creating its own plan for you, and chances are it won't be a plan you're going to enjoy. A life handed to you by default is rarely a meaningful, successful, or fulfilling life."

I thought about my old friends and how they never talked about their plans for the future. Well, except for being a professional baseball, football, or basketball player. Was society creating a plan for them?

"Well, I think I do plan ahead," I said. "I think about my future all the time. Is that what you mean?"

"Yes. That's exactly what I mean. How do you make your plans?"

I wasn't sure I wanted to tell him. I hadn't really ever told anyone about my plans, but I took a deep breath and started talking.

"Well, I have this thing called a Mission Statement." Granddaddy nodded his approval. "How'd you know to do that?"

"I found this book by Anthony Robbins and read about it in there. I thought it sounded like a cool idea so I wrote one. Now when I get up in the morning I read it before I do anything else. I also read it at night. It's the last thing I do before I turn out the light. Anthony says that doing this will program my mind for success."

"Great! What's your statement about?"

I shrugged. "It's just a few simple sentences about my goals and about the kind of person I want to be."

"How'd you decide what to write?"

"The book said to visualize the future I wanted, so every morning for the last couple of years while I was walking my morning paper route, I'd imagine what it would be like doing some of the things I really wanted to do... like making the varsity teams in both football and wrestling.

"And you know what? It's working! I've already made the varsity teams in both sports, and I'm just a sophomore in high school!"

"And you know what?" Granddaddy said. "You're using the exact same strategy Gretzky used. He skated to where he knew the puck would be. The puck wasn't there when he started moving, but he planned it just right, and the puck was there when he arrived. You're doing the same thing; turning the invisible into the visible by planning and then expecting to see it. You're pretty smart for a teenager."

I couldn't believe I was having this conversation.

People were always congratulating me and stuff, but I never talked about how good turning my dreams into reality felt. I didn't want to brag, but it didn't feel like bragging with Granddaddy.

"You know," he continued, "it's okay, Dakota, to feel good about what you've accomplished. You've done a good job. I've been very impressed with what you've achieved so far. I know you were the captain of your freshmen football team and you're the only sophomore on the varsity team right now."

I stared at him. How did he know that?

"Furthermore, I know that as a freshmen wrestler you lost your first wrestle-off to one of your team's returning varsity wrestlers. I know you broke the middle finger on your left hand during that wrestle-off and that you refused to take the school bus home. Instead, you walked the five miles. And when you thought nobody was watching, you cried out with the pain. If I know you as well as I think I might, it wasn't just because of the broken finger, it was because you lost your first wrestle-off."

"You saw that?" I asked feeling a little embarrassed.

"I did. I also know that even after the doctors told you you'd have to sit out most of the season, you kept learning, improving, and wrestling with that broken finger. If I'm remembering it right, it was only a few weeks later when you beat that same varsity wrestler in another wrestle-off. In fact, you continued beating him at every weekly wrestle- off. That's how you earned and kept earning your spot in the starting lineup on the varsity wrestling team as a freshman."

"How do you know all that?" I asked.

With his face visibly turning sad, Granddaddy responded, "Even though you haven't seen me around much, that doesn't mean I haven't been around and paying close attention to what's going on in your life."

"I never knew," I said. I wasn't sure how I felt about it, either. He had been there? He had seen me? It would have been so great to share my success with someone. "Why didn't you let me know? Why didn't you say something or let me know you were there?"

"Listen," Granddaddy started, his voice very serious, "sometimes things are complicated, and this is one of those times. At any rate, I'm here right now, so let's stay on track. You were telling me about how you visualized the invisible into the visible."

"Well, I visualized my goals so often, and they were so clear in my mind, I was able to break them down into small specific details and then fit them into a timeline. I had this past football season mapped out at least a year ahead of time. One of the things I visualized was our football team having a great season. Almost all of it turned out the way I had imagined too. We even made it to the playoffs. You're right... I made the invisible, visible.

"Yup. Good example."

"I've also been visualizing wrestling too. I'm expecting our wrestling team, and myself, to be very competitive and place in the state tournament this coming season. I can already see my junior year, and I've developed a sense of certainty that both the football and wrestling teams will go even further in the playoffs next year. For my senior year, I'm visualizing both teams being unstoppable and winning the state championships. Finally, I'm certain I'm going to win the individual state wrestling title at 145 pounds."

"Wow," Granddaddy said raising his eyebrows. "The 145-pound weight class is a pretty tough weight class. Aren't you wrestling in the 132 class this year?"

"Yup," I answered confidently.

"So, you're a sophomore in high school right now, and through this visualization you know how much you will weigh in two years when you're a senior?"

"Yup. In fact, I'm certain of it. Not only do I know how much I will weigh in two years, but I also know I'll be the captain of both the football and wrestling teams. And, I'll be the 145-pound state wrestling champ!" I suddenly realized that for the first time I was saying all of this out loud to someone. It was weird but it was also kind of easy because I really believed what I was saying.

I couldn't stop myself from talking. "I know it sounds like a lot, but I've been visualizing this for so long that it doesn't feel out of reach anymore. I expect to win and I do. I mean... don't get me wrong, I still get nervous before each wrestling match or football game, but it's different now. It feels like my destiny. All I have to do is follow my plans and the winning and success will continue. I know how it sounds, but what can I say? It's what I believe. It's what I know."

"The ancient Greeks called it hubris. We call it cockiness," Granddaddy said with a big smile on his face. "But you're right. What you're talking about is different, Dakota. Great people always start with absolute belief in their minds before they are great in the outside world. I like what I'm hearing, and I can see you're really fired up about this. It's impressive. You're a teenager and you already know how to write and use a mission statement. You've already figured out how to take your planning to the next level using visualizations, and it sounds like you already know how to use your visualizations to add details to your planning. Most adults don't know anything about either of those two strategies. But you keep right on doing what you've been doing."

"So you don't think it's too cocky to think that way?"

"No, I don't," Granddaddy replied without hesitation. "Contrary to what a lot of people think, success is not hubris or cockiness. We should all strive to live our lives to the fullest. Our forefathers, the Framers of our revered Constitution, understood this and made sure we'd all have the inalienable right to the pursuit of happiness. Being successful makes people feel happier and more fulfilled."

I thought about that.

"Look at it this way," he said. "If you don't make decisions about what you want to do or where you want to be in the future, then you're stuck back in that kayak without a paddle. So keep reading your mission statement. Put your emotions into it so you really feel it when you say those words. Keep visualizing and programming yourself for success. As long as you keep doing those things, I believe you'll not only fill the tall order you've written for yourself, but I also think you'll surprise yourself and achieve even more than you've ever dreamed!"

Granddaddy turned to face me. "The big trick for you right now is to carry that positive way of thinking, planning, and working over to the classroom. You've got to do better than those C's you've been getting."

My mouth opened, but nothing came out.

"Hey," Granddaddy said, "don't be so surprised. I told you... I've been paying attention. And now that we've been talking, I know you'll be able to figure out how to use a mission statement and visualizations to step up your class work too. By the time you master that, you'll be ready to start thinking and planning for your life way beyond school and sports. You're already having a positive effect on your teammates and your school with your success. Think of the impact you can make when you take all your skills out into the world."

"Wow!" I said. "That sounds really great... and kind of scary all at the same time."

"I think the word you're looking for is empowering," Granddaddy said.

"Yeah... You're right," I said nodding my head. "It's empowering. It's a lot to think about, but I like it."

THE PAIN OF REGRET

"People think it's too hard to do the extra work that's needed to excel. But what's really hard is living with the regret of knowing you could have done more."
—Daniel Blanchard

We were quiet for a while, listening to the rain.

"Now, getting back to talking about planning," Granddaddy said. "It's a sad truth, but very few people plan their lives, and that's one of the reasons there are so many people in this world living below their potential. I want to make sure you understand that people don't plan to fail in life on purpose. Most people just fail to plan. The trick is to not judge those people too quickly.

"Don't think people fail simply because they're unintelligent. There are brilliant people who never experience success and regular people who experience extraordinary success. The fact is, most people have never been told the secrets of how to succeed in life. No one helped them understand that they had options other than the ones they'd been surrounded with while they were growing up. That's one of the reasons I'm sharing these secrets with you today. I don't want you to end up like so many of your classmates will... living a life without direction or inspiration."

"I won't," I replied.

Granddaddy chuckled. "I know you won't, Dakota. But when you see it happen to someone you know, you might be tempted to think it's their own fault for not trying hard enough. Sometimes it's because no one ever took the time to teach them how. The secrets I'm teaching you today aren't taught in school. Most parents don't know them because they weren't taught them at home or in school when they were growing up, either.

"Today, kids are only getting a partial education at home, at school, and out in society. When your classmates grow up and become parents themselves, most of them still won't have heard any of these secrets. If they don't know them, then they won't be able to teach them to their kids, either.

"It's a cycle that keeps playing out, generation after generation of potentially great and fully capable children getting only portions of the knowledge they need to live the life of their dreams. Doesn't mean they won't try, but most will give up at some point and then end up living well below their true potential. Have you ever heard of the 80/20 rule?"

"No," I answered.

"Well, I'll start explaining it using your school as an example. I could say that 80 percent of the student body is made up of good kids who don't really cause any problems while the other 20 percent always seem to be getting in trouble. As a result, your school might get a bad reputation depending on how bad the 20 percent is.

"It can work in the other direction too, like with grades. Twenty percent of the students are getting the best grades. The kids in that higher 20-percent group are going beyond the call of duty and excelling at their class work. Think about what happens when they get out of school and get jobs. The 80/20 rule applies in the workplace too. There, the top 20 percent very often end up carrying the load for the 80 percent who've given up trying to get into the top 20 percent. Does that make sense?" Granddaddy quizzed.

"I think so. Now that I'm thinking about it, there are definitely athletes in my school who give everything they have. Maybe that's why they do better than the others," I replied.

"That's probably accurate," Granddaddy said. "What would you say if I told you 20 percent of the people in this world control about 80 percent of the money and resources?"

"Is that true?" I asked.

"It is. And it's not because the 20 percent is made up of people who know how to work the system or because they inherited all their money. A majority of the people in that 20 percent have worked long and hard for their success. The idea that they haven't is a cop-out people outside the 20 percent fall back on when they don't know how to bring more money or success into their own lives. Instead, they look at everything those other people have and complain that life just isn't fair."

Granddaddy shook his head. "Furthermore, those kinds of ideas are disempowering. So don't ever give in to the temptation of going down that road. If something in your life isn't working right, don't blame other people or the system. As soon as you start putting energy into blaming someone else, you aren't putting energy into doing something about it. Take responsibility for your own life and ownership of your energy so you get to be the one who decides where it will do the most good."

"Okay," I said. "I get what you're saying... Don't blame other people, or say that something isn't fair."

Granddaddy nodded and was quiet for a minute. "The other thing about people claiming that life isn't fair is that they'll say it when they don't feel like there's anything they can do. For example, did you know that one out of every two marriages ends up in divorce?" I shook my head.

"One of the biggest reasons people get divorced is because of money. When you first look at this problem, it's easy to look at the money issue and decide it's because one of them isn't working hard enough. But there are a lot of different ways money can play a role.

"Say the couple starts out okay, but then they have a baby and now they need more money than they have. Babies tend to cry a lot when they don't get their diapers changed. Diapers cost money, though, so maybe the parents can't change the diapers as often as they should because they can't afford to. Their baby keeps crying because he or she wants a dry diaper. It's a tough situation and extremely stressful for the parents. Some parents just don't know how to handle the stress and end up making terrible choices. All that stress is one of the reasons there are so many abused and neglected children in this world."

"Are diapers expensive?" I asked.

"Anything you need and don't have the money to buy becomes expensive in your mind. Money can become a huge stress producer for anyone, though—not just parents. That stress can lead to all kinds of bad choices. Is there any such thing as a happy, generous, kind, well-adjusted criminal who isn't out to make money?" Granddaddy shook his head.

"Money may not be the number-one reason people do bad things, but I bet it's in the top three."

My mouth tightened. "I didn't realize money was one of the reasons parents abuse their kids. I've heard Mom and Pops fighting over money, but... I—"

"Hold on. That's not exactly what I said. The point I was trying to make is that when it comes to money, people don't always make good decisions. When they make bad decisions, the people around them usually end up suffering with the consequences too. Money is not the only reason people struggle with being good parents. I just used that as an example to help you understand that having enough money is a problem a lot of people struggle with.

"For some people, money is an issue that never goes away. They don't realize there are other things they can do. They don't know other choices and options exist because no one ever took the time to explain them. They only know what's in their pocket. Even if you told them, a lot of those people are so used to having empty pockets and storm clouds hanging around them that it would take more than an idea to get them motivated."

I looked out at the clouds. They were moving fast now.

"You mean like those clouds out there?"

"In some ways, yes," he answered. "But if you notice, those same storm clouds are headed our way too."

As if on cue, the rain really started coming down.

"Everybody has storm clouds in their life," Granddaddy continued. "We've all experienced the unrelenting downpours that sometimes come along with them too. What I'm saying is that there are people who don't have the resources or know-how to protect themselves from the storms life sends their way. For them, those storms are a constant stress. One storm hits them and before they have a chance to recover from that one, another storm comes along."

The wind was picking up too. I moved a little closer to the center of the table to keep from getting wet.

"Those storms start invading their dreams and waking them up in the middle of the night. That kind of constant stress does something to people and they end up making even more bad choices. They might start putting on extra weight or become so grouchy or mean that they alienate their families and friends. They get angry and blame anything and everyone around them. Stress is a lot like a parasite. Once it takes hold, its roots dig deeper and deeper into a person's hopes and dreams."

"That's a pretty scary thought," I said.

"You're right. It is," Granddaddy agreed. "It's tough to handle life's storms when you don't feel like you have any options. Never-ending stress is one of the reasons many good and able people turn to overeating, smoking, alcohol, drugs, or even meaningless sex. Each one of those is a way of temporarily escaping the weight of all the storms and stress hanging over their heads. When people do these things they get to forget... at least for a little while... about the distance between who they are and who they might have been. Their vices are like temporary shelters against the constant onslaught of storms."

"I know some people who do drugs," I said. "They've tried to get me to do them too. They say it's fun."

"I don't doubt they say that. But let me ask you this. Are they people who have a plan?"

I thought about that for a minute. "I guess not, unless you consider figuring out how to get high without getting caught as a plan."

"Well, maybe you're right. That is a plan, but what do they get at the end of it? Nothing worth having. All those activities... drugs, alcohol, smoking, overeating, and promiscuous sex have a way of sucking the life right out of you. Eventually, people who use those things as a way of escaping their storms look in the mirror and see a person they barely recognize. Because they never knew there was another way, they'll cave into the idea that they're just another victim of a world that doesn't care. They'll surrender to their circumstances and give up the idea that there's anything they can do to change what's happened. They accept that they are helpless." I just stared at the floor.

"So here's the thing, Dakota. I'm not telling you this to make you feel bad. I'm telling you this so you can grasp how amazing the stuff you're doing really is. When your friends tried to get you to take drugs you could have said yes. But you didn't. You have plans and you chose to follow them instead. There might not be a lot of physical distance between you and the people you know who are doing drugs right now—some of them are probably sitting right next to you in school—but where will they be in ten years? Where will you be in ten years if you keep following your plans?"

"They'll be stuck in a kayak without a paddle heading for a waterfall?" I offered.

"Ah... you're paying attention," Granddaddy said with a smile on his face. "And when they are, they won't be in any position to help the others around them—not even their own children. So the 80/20 rule continues to exist because it gets passed on from one generation to the next. Dad doesn't know what a paddle is so he can't teach his son what a paddle is either.

"The sad thing is that everybody has the power to do something. Everybody. Most of the 80 percent have just stopped trying. They believe other people have all the power while they have none. In other words, they have become both helpless and hopeless. But it's easy to understand. None of their parents, friends, school guidance counselors, or college advisors knew there was anything to share beyond academia. Sadly, the conversation you and I are having is rare."

"Wow. Listen to you! You're all fired up today, Granddaddy!" The words had charged out of my mouth before I had a chance to think about how they might have sounded. "I'm sorry. I didn't mean to throw all that attitude your way. It's just that I can tell you feel very strongly about what you're saying... and I'm glad to be here and all... but why today? Why are you so fired up and insisting that I have to learn these secrets today? I mean..."

"Well, today is your birthday. And I know you don't know this, but 60 years ago today was also my 16th birthday. We have the same birthday!" Granddaddy announced proudly. "Sixty years ago today, I ran away from my hot-tempered, overbearing father. I lied about my age and joined the army-air force to fight against Hitler. Shortly after I enlisted, I met Colonel Reynolds of the 475th Fighter Group and my whole life changed. November 30th, 1941, was the most important day of my life. I chose to come here today to share with you what Colonel Reynolds shared with me."

"So today's your birthday too?"

"Yup. I kind of figured you didn't know."

"No... I didn't. Pretty cool, though. Happy Birthday, Granddaddy."

"Same to you," he said with a smile. "So that's why it had to be today. This day is very important to me, and hopefully it will be a day you'll never forget, either. Colonel Reynolds shared these secrets with me on a day very much like this, and now I get to pay it forward by sharing those secrets with you. My goal is that you'll always remember this day as the day someone took the time to share the secrets of life with you. This is a day that could change everything for you. By the time we're done, you might even look forward to the day when you get to pay it forward to someone else too."

My mind was racing and I could feel my heart beating. This felt right. I could just tell it was meant to happen. I wanted to say something but I didn't know what to say. Besides, I didn't want him to stop talking. I wanted to hear the secrets.

"Sixty-years ago today, I grabbed onto an opportunity and landed in the midst of some incredible men. These were men who had been tough enough to get through the Great Depression, win a two-front war against overwhelming odds, and later the men and women of their era would be called the Greatest Generation. I had the privilege of fighting alongside them under a couple of distinguished leaders named Colonel Reynolds and General Eisenhower. Together, we fought against another powerful and capable leader,

Hitler."

"I learned about Hitler."

"I'm sure you did, but books don't do a good job of explaining what he used his leadership to do. His leadership almost destroyed the world. Hitler viciously killed six million Jews. He was literally trying to exterminate an entire race of people. It was a terrible time, and even though I learned so many incredibly powerful secrets going through it, it took me a very long time to really understand them all.

"I tried to share some of them with my son... you know... your dad, but by the time I was able to figure out how to start explaining them, he was already past the point of being willing to listen to anything I had to say. It was a hard truth for me to accept, but there it was. I was too late to be the father and mentor he'd so desperately needed."

"What happened between you and Pops?" I quietly asked.

"That's complicated," Granddaddy answered. "I wasn't around much for him, and I know I haven't been around for you either, but there are reasons. And I know your dad has probably said some unpleasant things about me, but I'm here to tell you in person: I do have your best interest at heart. You're already headed in a good direction, but I don't have much time to share these secrets with you, and I do want to make sure you get the same life-changing information I got without having to go fight in a war to get it."

"What do you mean you don't have much time?" I protested. "You said this was our special day, and I thought we were spending the whole afternoon together. Where do you have to go?"

"That's not what I meant," Granddaddy said. "I promise you I'm not running out on you today, Dakota. I'm here to spend as much time with you as *you* have available before *you*

have to go to work. Wrestling season starts tomorrow, right?"
I nodded.

"Well, that means today is the only free day you're going
to have for quite a while. That's what I meant when I said I
don't have much time."

"Oh," I said and took a deep breath. "Hey, how'd you know
wrestling starts tomorrow?"

"I told you, I've been paying attention."

I looked down at my sneakers. We were about as far inside
the pavilion as we could get, but we were still getting hit by the
rain blowing in. "Boy, this pavilion sure is beat up. I hope the
roof stays on."

IT'S ALREADY IN YOU!

---

*"What lies behind you and what lies in front of you, pales
in comparison to what lies inside of you."*
—Ralph Waldo Emerson

Granddaddy looked down at his shoes. They were getting wet too, but he didn't seem to mind. "I think it'll hold. And yes, it might be old and beat up like this picnic table, but we're okay while we're in here. We don't always need as much as we think we do. As a matter of fact, wanting more is where most of our unhappiness comes from. Have you ever heard of Buddha?" "No," I replied.

"He introduced a simple concept that's been around for thousands of years, but most people don't seem to grasp who Buddha was or what his message was really about. Buddha taught people that the root of all unhappiness comes from wanting more and not being happy with what you have. He taught his followers that the true path to enlightenment is finding happiness with what you have. It isn't found at the end of a pursuit for what you don't have... but don't confuse what he said with complacency. We all still need to strive to do our best in life because when we do, we don't just improve the quality of our life, we also improve the quality of the lives of the people around us. If our efforts are based solely on gaining material possessions, we won't get the same results. For example, you've probably heard that I'm successful." "I've heard some things," I said with a smile.

Granddaddy chuckled. "I bet you have. But what kind of car do I drive? I drive a regular, every-day, ordinary car. I could easily afford a big expensive car, but I chose to drive an average car and live in an average house."

"I always wondered about that," I said. "If you really are as successful as Pops complained you are, then why don't you live in a big fancy house and drive a big fancy car like other successful people?"

"That's a good question, Dakota, and I have an answer, but I'd like to tell you more about how this all started for me first. Basically, I'm asking you to trust me the same way I trusted Colonel Reynolds when I met him on my 16th birthday," said Granddaddy.

"Sure," I said, nodding my head.

"Colonel Reynolds was a real man and a real leader. He was the kind of high quality person who only comes around once in a great while. His father was present at the 1914 Christmas Miracle of World War I and personally witnessed what destructive leadership was capable of doing. On Christmas day, the German and English soldiers stopped fighting and celebrated Christmas together in the middle of the battlefield in a space called 'No Man's Land.'

During their celebration, the enemies became friends and brothers and promised not to fight each other anymore. Unfortunately, their own officers had different plans. When their men refused to fight, they came down to the battlefield and forced the soldiers, at gunpoint, to break their promises and start killing each other again."

"That really stinks."

"You got that right. That Christmas Miracle could have ended World War I and possibly avoided World War II. It could have saved so many lives and put a stop to the immeasurable amount of misery and destruction war causes. It was a lesson in bad leadership that Colonel Reynolds' father never forgot. He in turn made sure his son learned it so he would always be able to tell the difference between good leadership and bad leadership.

"Great leaders like Colonel Reynolds get pushed to the front when they are needed the most—like during the war against Hitler. I was very grateful to have served under his leadership. He was an incredible man and the first person who ever took the time to tell me that if I wanted to be happy, then I should always strive to better myself. He'd say, 'Shoot for the stars and miss with the moon.' At first I didn't know what he meant. I'd heard the saying *Shoot for the moon. If you miss, at least you'll be among the stars*, but I'd never heard it the way he'd said it."

"That's the way I've heard it said too. Shoot for the moon," I said. "That's what I'm doing—shooting for the moon. Is that wrong?"

Granddaddy looked surprised. "Not at all. As long as you have a goal and you're taking steps to achieve your goal, you're going in the right direction. What Colonel Reynolds explained to me was that we get to pick our goals. I know it sounds easy, but too many times the goals we pick have all kinds of limits on them. Think about your own goals, the ones you told me about. I can tell you're very determined, but do the goals you've set reflect everything you've ever dreamt about? If you could dream bigger, what would you dream?"

I hesitated and then whispered my answer. "The Olympics."

Granddaddy nudged my shoulder. "Now that's the kind of dream Colonel Reynolds would be impressed with. I'm impressed with it too, Dakota. I'm also willing to bet that as you make your plans and work on achieving the goals you have right now, each one you accomplish moves you one step closer to being willing to consider the Olympics as an achievable goal rather than a pipe dream. Is that true?"

"Yeah, I guess so. I haven't really said it out loud to anyone before. It feels kind of weird."

"I can understand that. But here's what I want you to understand. You always want to have big dreams—dreams that are much further away than the moon. Our achievements are proof to our own selves of what we are capable of accomplishing. Our dreams give us a reason to continue reaching and striving beyond the goal we've just accomplished."

I nodded my head thoughtfully.

"When you reach for the stars, you'll have something to shoot for after you hit the moon. Another thing Colonel Reynolds said was, 'Pursue the abilities of the elite with unwavering determination.' He said that one a lot."

I chuckled. "That sounds like something my girlfriend would say. She's always telling me to *dare to dream* and that I could probably be better at a lot of things—like studying. She says I get too zoned in on some things and because of that, I don't put enough effort into others... That's also about the same time she puts her homework away so I can't see it. I don't think it's such a big deal. I get my homework done... most of the time."

"It sounds to me like you have a pretty special girlfriend," Granddaddy said, smiling.

"She's great. But she's a girl too, so you know what that means... complicated." I looked at Granddaddy hopefully. "Is that one of the secrets you're going to tell me today? How to deal with complicated women?"

Granddaddy smiled and shook his head. "No... we have enough to talk about without going there. But it's nice to know she cares enough about you to give you some grief when you're looking for shortcuts instead of doing the work."

"I don't take shortcuts. I work hard."

"Dakota, I don't think that's what she was saying and it isn't what I'm saying. Sometimes settling for less is a shortcut. For example, if your grades aren't where you'd like them to be, the difference between a B+ and a C- is a kind of shortcut. It takes less work to get a C-. Letting someone else do the work for you, well, that's a shortcut too. What would happen if you took a shortcut when you were lifting by cutting your reps in half so you'd have more time outside of the gym? What would happen? How far would the results of that kind of workout strategy take you?"

I grimaced. "Not very far."

"Think of how it would affect your ability to achieve your goals."

"It would make them impossible."

"Well, I don't know about impossible, but I agree with you in that it would make them almost impossible. So can you see that when you put your effort into things, you can accomplish a lot more?"

"Yeah... I can see how that works."

"Okay, if you want to develop a habit of success, then get in the habit of putting your full effort into the things you want to accomplish, even if you don't think it's that important at first. Everything you accomplish is a result of your effort. If you want better results, then make sure you're giving yourself a better chance to succeed by putting in the work. Be pleased with your accomplishment when you hit the moon, but don't stop there. There's only one moon.

There are lots of stars."

"Wow. That's a cool thought," I said.

"So is being an Olympian," Granddaddy said. "Have you thought about what your life will be like when you get there?" Granddaddy asked.

"I don't know. Maybe a little. I know it's going to take a lot of work to get there, but it'd be cool to have a nice car... I guess." "Yup... Cars are great," he said. "They can definitely take you places."

I thought about Granddaddy's car. It wasn't all that fancy. "So how come you don't drive a fancy car? I mean... I don't know... Maybe it's none of my business."

"No, it's okay to ask, but I'm going to answer the real question you were trying to ask. Yes, I could afford to drive any car I want. I did a long time ago, but if I had followed Colonel Reynolds's advice, I wouldn't have made that mistake."

"He said buying an expensive car is a mistake?"

"No, he didn't say that, but that's what I heard. What he said was to strive for greatness, but live an average man's life."

Granddaddy shook his head. "Believe me, I know how it sounds. I didn't get it at first, either. It seemed to me that if I was making the money to afford it, then what was the harm in spending it? I found out what he meant the hard way.

"I bought that fancy car and it was something to see. When I drove it off the lot I couldn't wait to drive down my street and have everybody see me driving that car. I was proud of it... proud of the fact that I could afford it. But after I drove down my street the first time, that was it. My neighbors and friends saw it, agreed it was a nice car, and that was it. No one talked about it after that."

"I don't get it. What's wrong with that?"

"There was nothing wrong with their reaction. It was my reaction that was the problem. I didn't want them to talk about how nice the car was. I wanted them to realize I could afford to buy it. I was finally making good money and that car was evidence of it. No one cared, though. In fact, it had the opposite effect. One of my neighbors even joked about me always buying stuff to show off. And then I understood what Colonel Reynolds was talking about. It's not about how much money you have that matters; it's what you do with it.

"People spend their money to prove they are richer than their neighbor. They hoard their money so they can have more money than their neighbor. They hide their money because they're afraid their neighbor might try to steal it. The whole time they are doing that, they aren't spending any time on being a good neighbor."

I smiled because I thought I understood the good neighbor part. It sounded a lot like what it was like to be on a team.

"As soon as I realized that," Granddaddy continued, "I stopped spending my money on things I didn't need and worked on being a better neighbor instead. Doing that didn't just make me a better person. It helped make me a wealthy person too."

"I think I know what you're talking about. That's what being on a team is like. You don't go around bragging about how good you are. If you do, your teammates aren't going to like it. But even when you don't brag, there are still going to be guys who look at you and think you're just lucky. During one football game I remember someone saying 'lucky catch' to me and it made me mad. I made that catch. Luck didn't have anything to do with it."

"It's good you know the difference. What some people call luck is actually when preparation meets opportunity. Most people think I'm very lucky. They think everything wonderful just drops into my lap, but there's a lot more to what they're thinking than that.

"People who don't know how to make things happen in their own life will often look at people who *are* making things happen and decide it's the result of luck. If they followed those successful people around, though, they'd see all the work it takes to be successful. But, for whatever reason, a lot of people aren't interested in doing the same amount of work. They'd rather believe someone else's success is the result of luck so they can still have a glimmer of hope for succeeding without doing any of the work."

I chuckled. "I had a senior once ask me how I got so jacked and I told him about my workouts. I even offered to show him, but he wasn't interested. I think he was trying to figure out what my weaknesses were anyway. I was kind of his competition."

Granddaddy nodded. "Yup, some people are like that. They don't want to do the work. But think about what happens to them. If they don't do the work, the only glimmer of hope they have to cling to *is* luck. Good preparation puts people in a position to be ready when opportunity knocks. Then, when opportunity does knock, they're able to do things... like making an amazing catch." "Do you know which catch I'm talking about?" I asked.

"I'm pretty sure. You've made a lot of great moves on the football field, but the one you're talking about was in the semifinal. What I want to make sure you realize is that the reason you were able to make that catch was because you put yourself in a position to make it. Luck didn't have anything to do with it! It was your preparation coming face-to-face with a real opportunity that you grabbed hold of. How many times have you done extra running and weightlifting outside of football or wrestling practice?" "A bunch," I moaned.

Granddaddy continued. "And when you made the varsity teams, I'm sure there were plenty of people who thought you made it onto those teams because you were lucky rather than because you are a focused, determined, and committed athlete. I bet there were people who thought you were lucky when you battled your way to placing in the state wrestling tournament at the varsity level when you were just a freshman too. You know different. You know how much work you do, and you know why you do it—so you'll be ready when opportunity knocks. But can you see the danger in believing that luck is part of why people succeed?"

I shrugged because I wasn't exactly sure what I believed about luck.

"The danger with believing in luck is that it can make you feel hopeless and helpless all at the same time. Anytime you look at something you or somebody else has accomplished and you take skill or effort out of the equation, you'll struggle with figuring out how to make it happen again. Think about the catch you made. If you really believed it when you heard the words 'lucky catch.' what are the chances of you being able to make that catch again?" "I'm not sure," I admitted.

"That's a good answer, and the reason you're not sure is because you used your skills to make that pivotal catch. If I take your skill and preparation out of the equation, I take away your confidence in your ability to do it again.

"People who believe they need luck to succeed, or decide that other people succeeded because they were lucky, are both helpless and hopeless. You can't prepare for luck. All you can do is sit and wait for it to strike. Even then, there's no guarantee it's going to come your way. People pray for luck when they don't have faith in their ability to make things happen. Does that make sense?"

"Yeah, it's like Gretzky... he wasn't lucky, he was prepared and ready to move to where the puck was going."

"Right! But think about the kayaker too."

"Okay... so he wasn't prepared... so he was relying on luck?" "Correct! Do you think the kayaker will try that again?"

"Doubtful. After going down the river without a paddle the first time, how would he know he could do it again without a paddle and still be okay?"

Granddaddy nodded his approval. "You know, I wasn't as smart as you are when I was your age, but I'm 76 years old today, and I'm here because every secret Colonel Reynolds shared with me was filled with truth. Every time I figured out how to apply one of the secrets he shared with me to my life, my life got better. I am living proof of the truth of his principles. Because of them, I am a happy person who has lived by a few simple principles while still leading a fulfilling, meaningful, and success-filled life. I want that for you too. I don't want you to ever doubt your ability to make things happen, but the hard truth is that I can only tell you about these secrets. I can't make you believe in them or use them."

It was still raining. We both stared out into the storm and saw a group of people running towards the parking lot. We stood and waved our arms and yelled, but they didn't seem to see or hear us. It was too bad because they still had a long way to go to get to the parking lot.

Watching them run past us got me thinking. This pavilion wasn't a fancy shelter, but it was keeping us safe and secure and that was all we really needed. The picnic table was in rough shape too, all scratched up from where kids had carved their names into it, but it was enough.

Those people were running to escape the storm, and they were running in the only direction they knew. They didn't stop or look around for any other possibilities. If they'd been looking around, they might have seen the pavilion and been able to get out of the rain, but none of them did. They just ran with their heads down, trying to escape the rain. I wondered where they'd run to if they were trying to escape one of life's storms. Would they rely on luck to help them? Would they be happy when they arrived at their destination? Would it be enough?

POPS OR DAD?

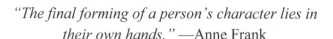

"The final forming of a person's character lies in their own hands." —Anne Frank

I stared out into the storm, mulling over the secrets Granddaddy was sharing with me. I don't know for how long, but then Granddaddy snapped me out of my trance. I turned towards him, not sure I'd heard him correctly.

"What?"

"Dakota, how's your dad doing?" Granddaddy repeated.

"You mean *Pops*?" I said, barely able to keep a tone of resentment out of my voice.

"Yeah, your father... How is he?" Granddaddy asked.

I could feel my lips pressing together. Why did Granddaddy have to bring him up? Up to this point we'd been having a nice talk. It was great listening to him and learning his secrets, but now he wanted to talk about someone I'd grown to hate. I didn't want to talk about Pops. What was I supposed to say anyway? Was I supposed to tell Granddaddy the truth? Did he really want to hear about all the times I'd been beaten—that we'd all been beaten?

Instead of answering, I shrugged. I could feel the weight of his stare pressing me for an answer, but I continued to stare at the floor. I remember reading somewhere that our eyes are a window to our soul, and I didn't want Granddaddy to look into my eyes and see how I really felt. After all, Pops was his son. I figured it might be hard for him to hear about how bad of a father his son had turned out to be. I didn't want to be reminded, either.

Then I wondered why I was trying to spare Granddaddy's feelings. If he knew so much, then he must know how Pops turned out. And if Pops is his son... well then how could he have let it all happen? How could he not know about the years of pain his son had caused his family?

Granddaddy finally broke the silence. "I know I haven't been around a lot."

"No, you haven't," I said, finally finding my voice.

"And maybe you'll say that because I haven't been around much it's none of my business, but I've always wondered why you call your father Pops. Every other father in our family is called Dad.

Why do you call your dad Pops?" "I don't know," I said shrugging again.

"Well, wouldn't you like to know?"

"I don't know... What difference does it make?"

"Maybe it doesn't make any difference, but let me put it to you this way, then. Why don't you call him Dad?"

I could feel the anger bubbling up inside me. I knew exactly why I didn't call him "Dad."

Granddaddy continued to question me. "I think you have a pretty good idea of why. What concerns me is that we can't talk about it. As long as you continue to ignore those reasons, or to examine them so you can understand them, they will continue to have influence over you and your life. Is that what you want?" "No! And let's be clear: Pops doesn't have any influence over my life. I am nothing like him and I'll never be anything like him." I stopped abruptly, my heart starting to race. I might not give two cents for what Pops thought about anything, but I did care about what Granddaddy would think if I kept going.

"I know that. And we aren't here to talk about him," Granddaddy said. "I have to confess I had an ulterior motive for asking you the question. I was trying to figure out how your relationship with him was going. I guess I got part of the answer. Your relationship with your father isn't any better. But you still haven't told me why you call him Pops instead of Dad."

I looked at him with my mouth wide open. "So you don't actually care how he's doing? You were just tricking me with a question?"

Granddaddy's expression turned serious. "No, like I said before, I'm not here to trick you into anything. But we have a limited amount of time to talk, so I want to make sure that what we do talk about is meaningful. I don't want you to have to wait years for some of these lessons to make sense. I understood many of the lessons Colonel Reynolds shared with me and was able to start applying some of them immediately. Others, though, took me years to figure out. Some I figured out way too late... like how to be a 'dad' to your father."

And then I blurted it out in a rush, "Because he's not my dad!"

Granddaddy looked surprised. "Now wait a minute, Dakota. I was there when you were born, and I can assure you that he's your Dad."

I shook my head defiantly. "No, you don't get what I mean. I know he's my father, but he's not my dad. A real dad would never treat his sons the way Pops treated me and my brother."

Granddaddy was nodding his head while staring at the floor.

"Like you said," I said, trying to stay calm, "you haven't been around. You don't know what it's been like watching that meanness change my brother. He's just as mean as Pops is now, and he's always in and out of jail. I just can't bring myself to call Pops something as nice as 'Dad' or 'Daddy'! It feels like a lie. 'Pops' is more neutral and unemotional. It's less endearing."

I took a deep breath trying to get away from the emotions that were getting in the way of me being able to stay calm. I hoped that if I stopped talking Granddaddy would break the silence, but he waited for me to keep going.

"Calling him Pops allows me to be civil with him when we interact. Maybe it isn't strictly true, but it helps me cope and get through it all, day after day. Calling him Dad would be a constant reminder of what he isn't, of who he'll never be, and of all the things I'll never be able to count on him for. That's why I don't let myself think of him as a real dad. He's not a real dad—at least not the kind of dad I wished I had. He's just Pops and I hope you're not expecting me to start calling him Dad."

"Nope... No expectation of that."

I breathed a sigh of relief and wiped my sweaty palms on my pants. I hadn't realized how fired up I'd gotten, and now I felt really self-conscious about all the things I'd just said. I'd never told anyone that before—maybe not even myself. It was beginning to feel like Granddaddy was putting me through the ringer, but I was willing to look at a few truths if it meant hearing the secrets he was sharing.

I remembered a teacher once saying that "to reveal is to heal," and I wondered if this was what he'd meant. Usually, I ignored my emotions and tried not to think too deeply about myself or the impact my surroundings have had on me. Instead, I'd learned to keep my emotions in check and not to let my weaknesses show. That went double when it came to Pops. There was no way I would ever be weak when it came to Pops.

"There is one thing I'd like you to consider, though," Granddaddy said. "There are a lot of people who call their fathers Pops, and it has the same meaning to them as the name Dad has to you. Calling him Pops instead of Dad won't change who he is, but it might influence the way you look at other fathers. And the truth is, you can't escape the reality of who he is by calling him by a different name."

I could feel my anger building, my blood pumping. I could call him anything I wanted to, and no one, not even Granddaddy, could change that.

"Do you know why I started lifting weights?" I asked. "I started lifting weights and wrestling so I would be strong enough to beat Pops up so he'd stop beating on us. I knew Mom couldn't stop him, and the police never did anything about it, so I figured I'd have to. I decided I was going to do whatever it took to get strong enough to force him to stop. But my brother beat me to it.

"Pops started wailing on him one day and he exploded like a trapped animal. He beat the heck out of Pops like I've never seen a person get beat before. I guess my big brother just couldn't take another night of the beatings. Things changed after that. After Pops's wounds healed, he tried to beat us a few more times before he figured out my brother was now the enforcer in our house.

"Unfortunately, my brother wasn't the same after that. It was like all of Pops' violence had rubbed off on him. Now he's always angry and so mean that he's ready to fight anybody who tells him what to do... including the police. Now he's in and out of jail like it has a revolving door. I still get so angry when I think about it. It was like he never had a chance."

"I'm really sorry that happened to your brother... and to you," Granddaddy said. When he continued, his voice was quiet and thoughtful. "A very wise man, Mohammed the Prophet, said: 'He is not strong and powerful who throweth people down, but he is strong who holdeth himself from anger.'"

I shook my head. "Don't worry," I said sarcastically. "I'm not going to throw your son down. I'll just keep calling him Pops. I'll keep my distance from him and I'll act civil towards him whether he deserves it or not." I was trying to sound calm, but without realizing I was doing it, I slammed my hand down on the picnic table hard enough to make it vibrate.

"Okay," he said. "I get that, and I know this is a tough subject, but I think you only heard the first part of what I said. You didn't hear the second part... 'but he is strong who holdeth himself from anger.' On your high school wrestling team you get rewarded for throwing people down, but in the real world there's no reward for throwing people down, even if you believe they deserve it. You saw what happened to your brother when he retaliated on your father and how it changed him. It didn't help him become a better person. What I hope you can see is that in your own way, you're doing the same thing, only instead of wrestling your father to the ground to make your point, you're calling him Pops instead of Dad."

I didn't want to, but I could feel the truth of what he was saying. "I... I can't. I just can't call him Dad... I can't."

Granddaddy put a hand on my shoulder. "I understand, and I don't expect you to call him Dad... He'd probably freak out if you did anyway. All I want you to think about is all the energy it's costing you to keep him in his place by calling him Pops. I'm willing to bet that every time you say it you feel a spike in anger. Do you want to feel that for the rest of your life? Will it be worth it if you end up carrying that anger around with you for the rest of your life? Please trust me when I say this: if you do, you will live to regret it."

And then he was quiet. Maybe Granddaddy had sensed he'd pushed me as far as he could with this subject. I wondered if I was stuck in a bizarre rerun of *Colombo*, the police detective show from the 70s we used to watch when we were growing up. Columbo was definitely a cool detective. He had a real talent for getting people to tell him what he wanted to know. He would emotionally push his suspects to the edge with his questions, get some information out of them, and then pull back just short of sending his suspects into a rage.

I suddenly wondered if that was Granddaddy's plan—to pull a "Columbo" on me. He had managed to get me to say a whole lot of things I would have never said voluntarily. He'd also gotten me to talk and think about the whole Pops thing without ever actually forcing me. Now he was tactically retreating. Was that his goal all along? If it was, he'd been successful. He'd shaken my beliefs, deftly planted a seed in my head about Pops and about not throwing people down in the real world, and then skillfully he'd stopped just short of me turning into a violent storm.

"Do you know who Socrates was?" Granddaddy asked breaking the silence.

Once again, Granddaddy had caught me off guard and I had to think about it for a minute. Yes, I did know who Socrates was. "Sure."

"Well, Socrates said a lot of things we still talk about today. What I like about Socrates is that if we're still talking about the things he was talking about thousands of years ago, then there's probably something to it... It means we aren't the first people to face these problems in our lives."

"Hmm," I mused. "I never thought about it like that. Do you think Socrates had issues with his dad too?"

Granddaddy chuckled. "I don't know... maybe. If he did, though, he must have come through them okay because he left us with some really great ideas to help us get past our problems. One of those ideas is that 'an unexamined life isn't worth living.' This is something we all need to do—we need to get to know ourselves and understand why we do the things we do. Lazy people don't do this. Neither do people who are afraid. Instead, they live their lives doing the same things over and over again because they haven't been able to find the courage to ask themselves the hard questions." I nodded my head agreeing with him. Talking about Pops was definitely hard, but I wasn't going to avoid it because I was afraid.

"That's one of the reasons I wanted to talk to you about your father. I wanted to help you figure out if you're ready to start taking the time to get to know yourself and understand why you do things. And I'm not saying there's a right or wrong answer here. There isn't. What I can tell you is that when you take the time to understand yourself, the quality of your life will improve dramatically. You'll be much more likely to live a life filled with things you chose to do rather than living a life where all you do is react to the things other people do."

I winced. Up to this point I thought I'd known why I did everything. I had a plan. I had a focus. Did I understand why? All this revealing was definitely not healing. Instead, it felt more like my feet had been knocked out from beneath me and I was heading face first for the mat.

"Listen kid, I know how hard some of this stuff is to talk about, but I promise it will make more sense as we go along. Examining your life isn't just about looking at the tough stuff. It's about looking at the good stuff too. All the stuff we've already talked about—like your plans and goals. All that stuff proves you're moving in a good direction. You're taking steps most grown men have never even considered and I'm really impressed by it."

I laughed. "Well I'm glad I got something right!"

"Oh come on now. Like I said, you've gotten a lot of things right."

"I don't know. Sometimes I feel so out of place it's really frustrating. It's not like there's anybody around who can relate to what I'm doing... Maybe I was born in the wrong generation. Maybe I should have been born when I could have been a part of your generation. Then I could have used my ability to fight for something good like fighting Hitler and making the world a better place to live—like you did."

"I guess you can look at it like that, but it won't change the fact that you're living now. Besides, you can do great things here just as easily. You already are."

I shrugged my shoulders and pondered what he'd said. I did have my sports, and instead of using all my strength, skills, and ability to defend myself against Pops, I was now using them to excel in the weight room, on the football field, and on the wrestling mat. But would I have any of it if my big brother hadn't stepped up?

"Maybe," I started, "but that wasn't my original plan. My first plan was to get strong enough to stop Pops. My brother just beat me to it. It was like he sacrificed himself for my mom and me. I didn't know he was going to do it, and I felt bad because he changed after that. Maybe if I could have helped him, things would've worked out differently for him."

"I can understand how you'd feel like that. It goes along with what you said about feeling like you might have been better off using your skills to help fight Hitler. It would have been different if you and your brother had been fighting side by side for something you both believed in. But I can just about guarantee that if you asked him if he would have wanted you to be a part of what happened, he'd say no."

"You think so?" I asked hopefully.

"Absolutely. That's why people step up and join the military or become leaders in the first place. They want to clear the path of opportunity for others. I can tell you with absolute certainty that he's proud of you even if he's never said it. And even though your relationship with him has changed, everything you achieve is evidence to him that what he did had value. Something good came out of a very bad situation."

"You really think he feels that way?" Granddaddy nodded.

I thought about that for a minute. "But we hardly ever talk."

"Families are tough sometimes. Maybe the best way you can honor his effort is by being grateful for both him and the path he cleared for you."

"I never would have thought of it like that. I've always felt guilty."

"Trust me, that's not what your brother wants either. That's not what people who pave the way want. It's certainly not what any soldier wants. All they want is for you to succeed."

"You know, when I realized I wasn't going to have to stop Pops, that was when I took all my intensity and started putting it all into sports instead. I guess you're right. If it hadn't been for my brother, I might not have made it this far."

Granddaddy nodded his head in agreement. "We all like to think our accomplishments are the result of our hard work and effort... and that's true, but it's also true that no one ever accomplishes anything without the aid and assistance of other people along the way. It's unfortunate that sometimes that aid and assistance is the result of a bad situation."

EVERY TRAGEDY INCLUDES
AN OPPORTUNITY

"When we meet real tragedy in life, we can react in two ways— either by losing hope and falling into self-destructive habits, or by using the challenge to find our inner strength. Thanks to the teachings of Buddha, I have been able to take this second way." —Dalai Lama

We were quiet again, the rain still coming down. I took a deep breath, trying to smell the storm. I couldn't decide if what I smelled was what a storm was supposed to smell like, but it smelled good all the same.

I wondered what Granddaddy was thinking about me. I was telling him stuff I'd never thought I'd say out loud to anyone. It felt strange because I've barely seen him over the years and hardly know him, but I still felt completely at ease with him.

"You know," Granddaddy said breaking the silence, "it takes a lot of courage, Dakota, to come through hard times. And I don't only mean the kind of courage that helps you make a touchdown or pin someone to the mat. You didn't crumple under the weight of what you went through. Instead you began working out and reading books. You searched for solutions to your unfortunate circumstances and found things to do to give yourself hope. You didn't give up on yourself! You didn't follow the footsteps of violence you found in your home and in the streets. You turned a terrible, negative environment into a powerful motivational force. Call it pay-back if you wish, but you decided that someday you would be the real deal, and that no one would be able to hold you down on the wrestling mat or in the real world." I nodded my head.

"I'm serious. History is filled with the names of successful people who grew up without the benefit of having someone standing nearby and cheering them on to victory. For example, when Napoleon was a little boy attending a military academy, one of his teachers made his life miserable." "Really?" I said surprised.

"Later, it was said that on his deathbed, Napoleon said, "I wonder what my old teacher thinks of me now?" I'd be willing to bet Napoleon also thought about what his teacher had said when his plans were executed to a victorious conclusion. And Napoleon is just one example of a reoccurring pattern throughout history, right up to today. Do you know who Michael Phelps is?"

"Sure," I replied. "He's an Olympic swimmer who represented the United States and won 18 gold medals between the 2008 and 2012 Summer Olympics."

"I'm not surprised you know that. Did you know that when a reporter asked him what drove him to be so successful, he said a teacher had once told him he'd never be successful? I guess he proved that teacher wrong.

"The Roman Emperor Marcus Aurelius said, 'A man's greatest tragedies usually lead to a man's greatest successes.' Knowing what those great men thought, I have to wonder how many of your victories were motivated by a desire to prove to everyone, including your father, that you could do it. That you weren't ever going to let anyone stop you from pursuing your goals without a fair fight."

I liked that Granddaddy said a "fair" fight. That was important to me. I was always aware of how strong I was and how easy it would be to push people around or intimidate them. At least with sports I can be strong without being considered a bully. If things had gone differently at home, that might have happened. But with sports, I don't have to think about what might have happened. I can be as strong and as skilled as I set my mind to be because it's always a fair fight. It's always a situation where I start out equal with my competition.

"You see," Granddaddy continued, "you have, in a strange sort of way, taken advantage of a gift many people are never aware of. You've taken the chaos and struggles you've experienced in your life and used them as inspiration to do and be more. You could have chosen to give up, but you didn't. Instead, you started designing your life for success and now your desire to succeed in life is a part of who you are. It's etched into your soul."

"My girlfriend is always saying that when life gives you lemons, you make lemonade."

"She's right! And it's good to remember your roots. We all start somewhere, and it doesn't do any good to fret about it after the fact. At that point, it's a history of factual events that took place. But that's when each of us gets to start asking better questions. What did I learn from the chaos of my past experience? How can I use my past experience to help me succeed in the future? How can I succeed in a way that makes the world better without falling under the weight of all the chaos around me?"

Granddaddy turned and looked at me. "You could have simply busied yourself with collecting trophies and medals. But again, you didn't. Maybe now's as good a time as any for you to acknowledge that you chose a different kind of future for yourself. You've experienced great tragedies, but now you've made a whole series of better choices and decisions and have been preparing yourself for success as a result. Your life has purpose now, and once you have a purpose and a plan... well... those are the roots of a meaningful life."

"You think I have a purpose?" I asked. "I've had people say things like that to me. Some people tell me I was born to wrestle, but I don't know. What do you think?"

"No one can tell you what you were born to do. That's something you get to decide as you set out on your own personal journey. Whatever you are focusing on at any given moment in time is your purpose in that moment. The more you learn about yourself, the easier it becomes to make decisions about what to do next. Right now, your past is a reminder of what you don't want. But as you continue pursuing your goals, your past will start filling up with things you feel good about too."

Granddaddy turned to look at me. "Dakota, this might sound like a weird question, but do you ever feel grateful for what you've accomplished?"

"What, like when I win at wrestling or get a good grade?"

"Kind of. Those are definitely things to be grateful for, but I was thinking more along the lines of being grateful to people who have helped you along the way."

"Sure. I'm grateful for my girlfriend and my coaches, I guess. It feels kind of weird to think about being grateful. I haven't thought about it like that before."

"People get confused about what it means to be grateful. Being grateful doesn't mean you owe somebody for something they did for you. Like if someone helped you finish your yard work so you could go out and do something else. It's more like you understand that if it weren't for what someone else did, you might not be where you are. No one makes it on their own. The more we understand that, the more likely we are to feel gratitude for the people who've helped us succeed, whether or not they are aware of the part they played in our success, even when it feels like they don't deserve it."

I shook my head. "You're talking about Pops again, right?"

"Maybe. Give it a shot. See if you can come up with a reason to be grateful when it comes to your father."

I sighed. "Okay. First of all, I hope you're not expecting me to be grateful for what he did."

"Nope."

"Good." I tried to think of why I would be grateful for him, but I was having trouble.

After a couple of minutes, Granddaddy broke the silence. "Don't focus on what he did or didn't do."

"What else is there to focus on?" I asked.

"You tell me."

If I took all the beatings out of the picture, there wasn't much left. I didn't really know Pops any other way. The only other thing he did for me was to help create me. I groaned.

"I got it. He helped make me. I wouldn't be here if it weren't for him."

Granddaddy smiled. "That's definitely something to be grateful for. One of the reasons you're here, right now, sharing all these secrets with me, is because of your father. I can honestly say *I'm* grateful for that. Let me ask you a different question. How do you feel about yourself as a person?"

"Okay... that's a weird question. I'm not conceited or anything like that... at least, I don't think I am."

"From what I've seen, you aren't conceited or self-centered. But think about your strengths too. Think about what you've accomplished so far even with all the bad stuff you've experienced. You're strong, you have a good work ethic, you don't quit when things get tough, and you know how to work through things even when they're tough to get through."

"I try to do those things for sure," I said trying not to sound as puffed up as what Granddaddy was saying about me was making me feel.

"Now, I don't know if your father has any of those traits, but your life might not be going in such a good direction if it had been different... if it had been easier. All your strengths and abilities have developed the way they have as a result of the way you've grown up so far. If you'd been a different kind of person, you might have ended up like other people who've experienced the same kinds of hardships. They spend most of their time complaining about how bad their life is and then give up the idea that they can have a better life. They don't look for things to be grateful for, so they never find them. Every success you experience has its roots in your past. Every good thing you have in your life has its roots in your past. You may not like your past, or the people in your past, but you wouldn't be here, right now, if it weren't for your past."

"You're killing me here," I said. "I've spent my whole life doing everything I could to stay away from everything you're talking about—including Pops. But now... and I get that I can be grateful that he helped make me, but I'm still not talking to him. I'm not going to run home and thank him."

"That's fine. I wouldn't expect you to. But I'll warn you right now, gratitude has a way of sneaking up on you. And now that we've been talking about it, you're going to start seeing some of the people in your life differently. That's what happened with me and my father."

"What?" I asked. "Really?"

"It's like I told you, I ran away when I was 16 to join the military. I had to get away from my father too. But years later, after I started to truly understand the power of gratitude, it was easier for me to think about him. And then I discovered something really interesting about gratitude. It doesn't take anywhere near as much energy to be grateful and forgiving as it does to keep your distance and to constantly have your guard up."

"You should have told me to bring a notebook. I don't know how I'm going to remember all this stuff!"

"Don't worry. You won't need to write it down. These secrets are the kind of stuff you won't forget. But you're right, we have been going through a lot of stuff. How are you doing with all this talking?"

"Well... it's definitely weird looking back at things because now they feel different... like the whole situation with my brother. I'm guessing that after I think about him for a while I'm going to be grateful for him too." I shook my head in com-

plete disbelief at what was going on inside my head. But somehow I knew it was going to be okay. I looked at Granddaddy
and smiled. "I'm doing okay."

WHAT'S IN A NAME?

> *"He who does not trust enough, will not be trusted."*
> —Lao Tzu

"I'm glad to hear it because I have another question to ask you." "I hope it's an easy one," I groaned.

"The first time you ask yourself any question, it can be a bit of a struggle. Sometimes the questions we need to answer make us squirm because they force us to look a little deeper. So I can't promise this question is going to be any easier than the last, but if you want me to stop. I will."

"NO!" I shouted and then immediately calmed my voice down. "No. I want to keep going. Ask me."

"I'd like to know why you don't ever call anybody by their name, Dakota."

"What? I don't understand."

"Like I told you before, I've been around even though you weren't aware of it." Granddaddy leaned towards me like he didn't want anybody else to hear what he was going to say next. "Part of my military training included learning how to blend into my surroundings without people noticing me."

"I don't get it. Why didn't you want me to know you were there?" I said.

"That's a very complicated question to answer, and I hope you'll find it within yourself to trust me when I say that it was always for your own benefit. Can you do that?"

I hesitated because I really did want to know, but then I shrugged. "I guess so."

"Good... now back to the question I asked. Do you know that in all the times I've heard you talking with people, I've never, ever heard you call anybody by their name? You always refer to people by their relationship to you."

I frowned. "I don't do that."

Granddaddy nodded his head. "Yes, you do, and it worries me. For example, you've been dating the same girl for a year now, so I'm figuring she's one of the most important people in your life, and yet you always refer to her as your girlfriend. That's how you've referred to her today—as your girlfriend. You haven't said her name once."

I sat and thought about what he was saying. Was he right? Maybe he was right. Maybe I didn't call people by their names. It seemed like a crazy thing to do because I know how much I enjoyed hearing my name, especially when it was for something like scoring a touchdown or a pin. I loved it!

Then I remembered a stupid etiquette class I'd sat through as a freshman where the teacher had said that we should always try to use people's names when we talk to them. It was a sign of respect. Rats! Now Granddaddy was going to expect me to be able to explain why I was doing this.

"Oh boy!" I sighed heavily. "Here comes the pain of getting to know myself again. Well, here goes nothing! Maybe I do it to protect myself?"

"Are you asking me a question or telling me why you do it?"

The Storm

"I'm not really sure. I've never thought about it before. Give me a minute."

"Take all the time you need," Granddaddy said.

I thought about the people we'd been talking about. He was right. It was always "my girlfriend" or "my big brother" or "one of my teammates," but I was stuck. I couldn't come up with a reason. "I give up. Tell me why," I said.

"You think I know?" Granddaddy laughed. "I don't know why—only you know why, Dakota. The thing I know is that people very often start doing something a certain way and then they keep doing it the same way until they come up with a better reason not to do it. So maybe you started referring to one person like this, it became a habit, and you started doing it with everyone."

"You think it's because I started calling Pops *Pops* instead of *Dad*, don't you?" Granddaddy shrugged.

I shook my head. "Look, I know you say you've been around, but being at my football games and wrestling matches isn't the same as being in my house. It's different there, and I had to do what I had to do to keep my distance from him. I had to protect myself and that was one of the ways I did it—by calling him Pops. I should have been able to trust him, to rely on him, and I couldn't."

I could feel my throat getting tight and took a few seconds to regain my control. "I had to do things to stop myself from hoping he'd ever change. It wasn't going to happen. As long as I call him Pops, I won't forget what he's really like or that he's not a good dad, and then he won't be able to hurt me any-more than he already has." "I can understand that. It makes a lot of sense."

Granddaddy waited a bit before continuing. "Is there any possibility you don't call other people by their names because you're afraid they might betray you too? The way your father did?"

"I don't know... maybe," I said, a hint of a whine entering my voice. "Can't you just tell me what you think?"

"Look," Granddaddy continued, "every reason you do something isn't automatically a bad reason. I understand why you call your father Pops. And you came up with the idea that you might be doing it with other people as a way of protecting yourself."

"I know, but do you think that's why I'm doing it?" I asked.

"Let's look at it. You call your father Pops to protect your-self from him. And like I said, people tend to do the same things over and over again, so yeah, I think it's possible you don't refer to people by name as a way of protecting yourself."

"It makes sense... I think."

"I also said people can change when they have a really good reason. So let me ask you. Do you think your girlfriend is going to betray you?"

"No!" I answered emphatically.

"I agree with you. I don't think she will, either," Grand-daddy answered. "But trust is a two-way street. If you don't trust and respect her enough to talk about her using her name, how does she know she can trust and respect you?"

"I never thought about it that way," I said, shaking my head.

"Using someone's name is a sign of respect. It feels good when people say your name. I'm sure you can relate to that. I've heard your name over the loudspeaker plenty of times, and I've seen you smile when you hear it."

I looked down, trying to hide the smile on my face. He was right. I liked it a lot.

"It's too soon to tell if she's the girl you're going to stick with, but if she is, she'll be there to protect you too. She'll even protect you from yourself when it's necessary! That alone should earn your respect. You know, I probably wouldn't have achieved anywhere near as much as I have if it wasn't for your grandmother. I know she seems like the quiet passive type, but believe me, she's every bit as strong as I am. Granted, she can't lift as much weight as I can, but she is stronger than I could ever be in so many ways. I owe everything to her."

"Wow, I never knew," I replied.

"She sees and hears things I miss. She's great at reading people's faces. She has a tremendous amount of patience, which she's needed living with me, but she's never done or said anything that wasn't in my best interest. She's picked me up when I've fallen and redirected me when I've lost my way. She's also protected me from myself, especially when I was blind to the obvious. Like your girlfriend, she too occasionally fumbles through her purse looking for her keys... and I agree with you, it's cute. I love your grandmother with all my heart."

Granddaddy sat with a smile on his face and looked like he was lost in thought. Then he cleared his throat and continued. "I don't know if your girlfriend will turn out to be your lifelong love, but I can tell you that your relationship will only grow as far as your trust and respect for her will allow. If you don't trust her enough to open up and be your whole self around her, then you'll never know if she's the right one or not. Just as important, though, is for you to trust yourself enough to let her be her whole self with you. People are a lot like puzzles when it comes to love. We each have a whole lot of pieces, but when they fit together, we can create something really great."

"I get what you're saying, but what happens if I trust her and it turns out she's not the right one?"

"There are a couple of ways to answer that. One is with the phrase 'nothing ventured, nothing gained.' The other is with the phrase 'with great risk comes great reward.'"

"I've heard both of those."

Granddaddy nodded his approval. "Okay. Then I don't have to explain that this is one of those times when you get to decide how you want to proceed. Will you settle for what you've got? Or will you reach for something better?"

I thought about it for a couple of seconds and quietly said, "Her name is Jenn." I was surprised at how it felt to say that. It felt really good. Then I turned to Granddaddy, feeling the smile on my own face. "My girlfriend's name is Jenn."

ATTITUDE OF GRATITUDE

> *"Reflect upon your present blessings, of which every man has plenty; not on your past misfortunes, of which all men have some."*
> —Charles Dickens

"Her name is Jenn," Granddaddy said, turning and smiling at me. "Thanks for sharing her name with me." "You're welcome," I responded.

"Of course, I have to confess that I already knew her name," he said.

"Yeah. I kinda figured you did."

"But thank you anyway," he said. "Thank you, Dakota, for finally trusting me enough to share her name with me. That's another step towards your Kaizen."

"My Kai... what?" I asked with a confused look on my face.

"Don't worry about that right now. We'll get to it soon enough. First, though, I want to talk about what I did after you told me Jenn's name."

"Okay," I said a little unsure of what Granddaddy was talking about.

"What did I do after you told me Jenn's name?" Granddaddy asked.

"I don't know," I replied with a shrug. "Did you do something?"

"Sure I did," Granddaddy said. "The problem is that what I did is so simple that most people would miss it simply because they aren't paying attention. But I'm willing to bet that if you take a minute, you'll remember. Think about it. You turned to me with a big smile on your face and said, 'My girlfriend's name is Jenn.' Then I..."

"I don't remember you doing anything specific. Maybe you turned towards me a little and smiled? Is that what you're talking about?"

"You're getting close, and you're definitely good at observing people's physical movements, but I did more than turn towards you and smile. In some ways, I'm not surprised you didn't catch it. You probably don't experience what I did on a daily basis."

"Well, if I don't know what it is, how can I tell you what it is?" I asked.

Sensing my frustration, Granddaddy calmly said, "I wouldn't be asking the question if I wasn't sure you already knew the answer. You do know. You just don't know you know."

I shook my head. I didn't want to disagree with him, but I honestly didn't know what he expected me to say.

Granddaddy continued. "I know how it sounds, but psychologically speaking, even though your conscious mind has already moved on and is paying attention to what I'm saying right now, your subconscious mind recorded and stored what happened. It did that for you because it knows your conscious mind can only pay attention to so many things in any given moment, usually seven things—plus or minus a couple. Your subconscious mind, on the other hand, is limitless. It never misses a thing. It's like a 360-degree movie camera that's always running, only there's no director telling it what to record. Instead, it records everything it witnesses. To access it, all you have to do is find a way to play back the recording."

I had an idea. "We learned about hypnosis in one of my classes.

Is that what you're talking about?"

"Hypnosis is definitely one of the ways people can gain access to what's been stored in their subconscious mind, but in a situation like this one, where I'm asking you to tell me about something that happened a couple of minutes ago, it's not really necessary. But getting yourself into the right state of mind will help. It's a pretty basic psychological tactic. Want to try it?"

"Sure... So... you're not going to hypnotize me?"

Granddaddy chuckled. "Let's try this first."

"Okay, but could you hypnotize me if you wanted to?" I asked eagerly.

"Probably," Granddaddy said with a mischievous smile. "Okay... Take a deep breath and let it out slowly." The tone of his voice was changing as he spoke, becoming calmer and slower. "Close your eyes... relax... and take another deep breath... slowly letting it out."

I followed his instructions and felt myself relaxing.

"Listen to the rain... You've been hearing it since we sat down... the steady pitter-patter of it hitting the roof above us. Feel the cool air as it blows through the pavilion carrying light drops of rain along with it. We don't mind the rain, though, because we're enjoying the conversation. I was telling you about how much your Grandmother means to me. You thought about it and decided to tell me your girlfriend's name. You turned to me with a smile and said, 'My girlfriend's name is Jenn'... then I... " Granddaddy let his voice trail off.

"Then you turned towards me... and smiled... and said thanks?" I opened my eyes and looked at Granddaddy.

"Did I get it right? Is that what you said?"

"Very good. I did say thanks. Actually I said, 'Thanks for telling me her name was Jenn,' but you got the part I was hoping you would. You remembered that I said thanks. Like I said, it was a very simple thing, but sometimes the simplest things are the toughest to grab a hold of. I also told you that you already knew the answer. The reason I wanted you to remember it on your own was partly because I wanted to prove to you that you could, but I also wanted you to remember what it felt like to hear me express my gratitude for sharing Jenn's name with me. Thanks and thank you are very powerful words. I made it even more powerful by clearly directing my thanks right to you when I turned and smiled. I also looked you right in the eye when I said it."

"Yeah, I remember that part now. Maybe that's why I was having a hard time remembering it. It felt a little weird, actually."

"I get that. It's tough for a guy your age to think about making eye contact. It isn't always safe to do it in the streets. I bet you do it when you're sizing up your competition in sports, though."

"Sure do. I'm not afraid of the competition and I want to make sure they know it."

"Did you know that studies show that it's not what you say, but rather *how* you say it that counts for about 55 percent of what a person notices and then feels about you?" Granddaddy asked. "That's what you're doing when you look your competition in the eye. You're showing them you're confident. That's 100 percent body language. When I said thanks, I used my body language in addition to my words as another way of making sure you knew I was genuinely grateful."

"I didn't realize I was using body language like that."

"We're always using our body language. Once you start paying attention to other people's body language, you'll be amazed at what you learn. It goes back to the whole thing I was saying about your subconscious. Even when you aren't paying attention, your subconscious mind will step in and pay attention for you. So you're already reading and reacting to people's body language, but right now it's mostly with your subconscious mind. For example, I bet you know what kind of mood Jenn is in without her having to say anything."

"Well... yes and no. I can tell when she's in a mood. I just don't always know why."

Granddaddy laughed. "Yes, but you can tell something is going on. I bet she can read your body language too. You can do a lot with body language—especially because most people aren't paying attention. Instead, their subconscious mind is paying attention for them, and they end up responding to someone's body language without even realizing they're doing it. You can actually use your body language to encourage people to trust you and treat you well. When you exude confidence and happiness and an attitude of gratitude it will show, and people will be more likely to like you, respect you, and want to be around you." "Hmm," I murmured. "You sure do know a lot about people. I had no idea I was using my body language like that."

"Oh, trust me, you knew it. It was just so natural for you that you never realized it. See, we learn these kinds of things by steps. As soon as we master the first step, we're ready to take the next step. You've already had an introduction to some of the things we've been talking about. Today, you're achieving a deeper level of understanding for some of the ideas you've already been applying to your life. For example, you just learned more about how body language works while you were gaining a deeper understanding of gratitude and how important gratitude is. Each step you take will aid you as you move towards your Kaizen."

"You said that word again. Are you going to tell me what it is?"

"Yes. In time I'll explain it to you, Dakota, but not right this minute," Granddaddy replied. "First, I have something else I'd like to share about gratitude."

"I get it, Granddaddy. Be grateful," I said, impatient to talk about something more interesting.

"You understand one aspect of gratitude. But understanding gratitude is like understanding anything else. It's a step-by-step process. When you were growing up, you learned how to crawl first, then you learned how to walk, and before you knew it, you were running. But you didn't start with running. You started with crawling and built up to it. Understanding the secrets we're talking about today works the same way. You'll understand the general idea, but as you learn more, you'll be taking bigger steps. Each step successfully taken gives you confidence to take the next step—even if you fail. Have you ever watched a toddler trying to stand and walk the first few times?"

"Yeah, my girlfriend... I mean *Jenn*, is an aunt and we watched her niece trying to walk one day. It was pretty funny. She fell a lot." "Maybe so, but did she quit?" I shook my head no.

"Of course she didn't. If she had, she wouldn't be walking now. She didn't stop after each fall and think to herself 'I'm never going to master this, it's too hard!' Instead, she kept right on working at it. Too many people take one step, fail, and then never find the courage to try taking another step. They've forgotten what it was like to be two years old and fearless. Instead, they're afraid people will think they're stupid for trying something new. Or they're too proud to let other people see them struggle. Or they're too concerned about what people will think of them if they fail. People waste a lot of time and a lot of life when they give into those excuses. We all make mistakes and fail along the way, but when we do, we can use that information to increase our chances of succeeding when we're ready to try again."

"I get the whole crawl-before-you-can-walk thing, but how can I fail with gratitude? I already know how to say thank you." "And it's easy enough to say thank you," Granddaddy said. "But that's only one part—one step. The next step is to realize that we are surrounded by things to be grateful for, every minute of every day. Remember when you asked me about my house and my car?" I nodded.

"I'm grateful for both of them. They may not seem extraordinary to your eyes, but to mine they provide comfort and shelter and a sense of security for me and your grandmother. We're grateful for what we have and don't need or desire more than what we have. Sometimes people who are always thinking about buying a bigger house or car haven't stopped to consider whether or not they're grateful for what they already have. If they did stop to feel grateful, they'd also have to stop and ask themselves why they want more. The point is, if you move forward with the idea that you're always on the lookout for more ways to experience gratitude, you'll never run out of reasons, people, or things to be grateful for."

I gave him a skeptical look.

Granddaddy nodded. "Okay, let me try to explain what gratitude really feels like."

I watched him close his eyes, take a deep breath, and smile to himself.

"When I start thinking about everything I'm grateful for, it fills me up to the point where I could explode with gratitude and happiness. Like sitting here and talking with you. I'm very grateful for this time, but I'm also extremely grateful for everything that led me here. What I want you to understand is that the only way I could be here is because my past led me here. And I wouldn't trade this time for anything."

Granddaddy opened his eyes and looked at me. "Don't get me wrong. I've had tough times too, just like everybody else. I just choose to learn from my mistakes and failures, and to be grateful for everything and everyone who's helped me along the way. When I look back at my life, I choose to remember the lessons I learned and all the situations that have provided me with opportunities to be grateful. I let go of the rest.

"As your understanding of the role gratitude plays in your life deepens, remember that no one accomplishes anything alone. Whenever you accomplish anything, you can start by being grateful for the knowledge and skill you used to make it happen, but make sure you start looking around too. As soon as you do, you'll quickly begin to realize how much help you've gotten along the way."

I thought about that and realized I knew exactly what he was talking about. "You mean like when I wrestle and I know my girlfriend's... sorry, I mean *Jenn's* there. I'm too focused to look her way, but knowing she's there makes a difference."

"I bet it does. The question is, do you say thank you to her for being there?"

That was a tough question, but not because I didn't know the answer. I did. "No... not really. I smile at her and I think she knows I'm glad she's there, but I don't think I've ever actually said the words."

Granddaddy was nodding his head and then asked, "How do you think she'd feel if you did?" I couldn't help but smile.

"Good."

"You're smiling thinking about it so I know you're getting it. Most people don't realize how great it feels to express their gratitude. If they did, they'd do it all the time because it's contagious. It's like tossing a tiny pebble into a lake. When the pebble hits the water, it starts a chain of reactions beginning with the first water molecules the pebble comes in contact with. Those molecules pass their reaction along to the next. We see the result as circular rings expanding and growing well beyond the point of impact, all from one tiny pebble." "Wow." That was all I could say.

"Wow is right. It's almost like magic and yet most people miss it because they don't think in terms of gratitude. In fact, if someone genuinely expresses gratitude to them, they get uncomfortable. They don't even know how to react. Like you didn't when I said thanks for telling me Jenn's name. Gratitude can and will improve the quality of your life... if you let it. You don't have to start with grand gestures, either. Simply start by looking for things to be grateful for. Once you get used to doing that, start figuring out how to express it."

I turned to Granddaddy and looked him right in the eye. "Thanks for being here today." It took every ounce of my strength to hold his gaze, but I did.

Granddaddy clapped a hand on my shoulder and with genuine warmth said, "You're welcome."

He was right. It felt really good. Strange, but really good.

DO THE WORK!

"A dream doesn't become reality through magic; it takes sweat, determination, and hard work." —Colin Powell

"Granddaddy?" I started. "Can I ask you a question?"

"Of course, Dakota."

"How do you remember all this stuff? It's like you know all these things. You talk about people I've barely ever heard of."

Granddaddy sighed and nodded. "I know it might sound like I know a lot, but you have to remember I'm a lot older than you.

You also need to understand that I sought out knowledge too."

"You studied?"

"Kind of. But it's more like reading books about things and people that interested me. For example, we've been talking about gratitude. When I first heard the idea, I wanted to know more so I started doing a little research. Know what I found out?" I shook my head no.

"I found out that a man named Cicero said that gratitude wasn't just the greatest of virtues, but that it was the parent of all other virtues. What's really amazing is that he said it over 2,000 years ago. He lived before Jesus Christ."

"So you studied Cicero?"

"Yes. I decided I wanted to know more about him. He lived so long ago and yet the things he said were relevant to me. His ideas made sense to me, and I liked the thought of having something in common with someone who lived so long ago. Just out of curiosity, have you heard of him or read about him in school?"

"Maybe. I think I remember his name from world history. Was he a Roman or something?"

Granddaddy chuckled. "Oh he was definitely a Roman, but he was a great speaker and today he's considered one of the most versatile minds to ever grace ancient Rome."

"Sorry. I guess I don't remember what we learned about him.

But I'm pretty sure it didn't have anything to do with gratitude."

"I'm not surprised. Today's history books don't seem to contain much more than facts and dates. They tell the facts of what men and women did, but don't include the details about who they were as people. We don't get to read their stories, so we don't have enough information to know what they were thinking, or truly understand the reasons that inspired their actions.

"It's sad too because those people had struggles in their lives just like you and I have in ours. I always wonder how much more interested kids in school would be if they stopped to realize that every historical figure they're reading about was a teenager once upon a time too. Take Joan of Arc for example.

She was 13 years old when she started having visions of driving the English out of France. When she was 16, she made her way to the French Royal Court and convinced the disinherited French crown prince, Charles of Valois, to let her lead his forces against the English. At 17, she won a series of battles and honored her promise to Charles of seeing him crowned king."

"We were just talking about Cicero," Granddaddy continued. "This amazing man was once the same age as you are right now. Wouldn't you love to know how he came up with all his great ideas? I wonder who he sat down and talked with. Was there someone like Colonel Reynolds in his life too?"

"Yeah... Or maybe he sat down and talked with his Granddaddy," I offered enthusiastically.

"Maybe," Granddaddy mused. "We can learn so much more from history than facts. It seems to me it's a challenge for students to get inspired by memorizing a bunch of dates."

"I can tell you from experience that dates aren't inspiring. They're boring. All they are is the difference between an A, a B, a C, or whatever."

I looked at Granddaddy. "Do you think it will ever change?"

Granddaddy looked thoughtful. "I'd like to think it would. I'd like to think the people who write history books will figure out that most of us get inspired by people, not by the date and time those people did something. Take movies for example. There are a lot of historical movies that are historically accurate and really inspiring. The actors in those movies aren't talking about dates. They're showing us what else was going on during that time, and we get to live through those historical points in time with them.

"Movie makers know how to keep us interested. They tell us more about what was really going on with those people. Sometimes they help us see the good guys succeed and the bad guys fail. If a director has done a good job, we might even have learned a lesson, or have gotten some information that might help us avoid making mistakes in our own lives. A really good, historically accurate movie might even inspire us to do more with our lives."

"They should make a history class like that—all movies. That would be a great class and we'd get to know more about the people in the process," I said.

Granddaddy shrugged. "You might be right, Dakota, but even if they talked about it, it's doubtful the decision-makers would agree on which movies to show. There'd be too many opposing opinions. They'd disagree on how much information to give you, or about whether or not you have a right to hear both sides of a story. They'd argue about how much of the story you should be exposed to, and there'd be times when they'd make decisions believing you need to be protected from the whole truth.

"Those are just a few of the reasons why you only get the information you get right now... a lot of bare-bones dates and facts rather than the whole story. I wish they'd give you more information. I think it'd be very powerful for young people to realize how young some of the greatest leaders the world has ever known were when they were making decisions that changed the course of history."

"It would be easier on the teachers too, I bet," I said.

Granddaddy cocked his head to the side and looked at me.

I shrugged. "I've overheard teachers talking about how hard it is to keep up with all the things they have to do. They get stressed about all the testing, and then they stress us out with everything they expect us to learn. It's not like it's a secret."

"They do expect a lot from teachers these days. They expect them to stay inspired, and then expect them to inspire their students while following curriculum restrictions that limit what they can teach. But... that's a topic for another day. What I hope you will take away from this is that just because your teachers aren't able to dive into the details, that doesn't mean you can't.

"You have a choice. You can walk away from your classes satisfied with having learned enough information to pass your tests, or you can take notice of the people and events that sound interesting to you and check them out on your own. And not just in history class either. You'll hear about amazing people in your other classes too. Look at it this way, every person who made it into one of your school books has a story to tell. If the results sound interesting, no one's going to stop you from checking the whole story out on your own."

"Maybe, but doing more homework by choice?" I moaned. "I don't know."

Granddaddy laughed. "I'm not saying to check out every person you read about. Just take a minute to ask yourself how a regular person... someone like you... could end up where they ended up. If you realize you'd really like to know the answer, check them out. It's easy enough to do with the Internet."

I nodded. "I guess I could do that."

"Good. It's important to study successful people. The cool thing is that successful people want you to succeed too. They don't want you to struggle like they did. That's why their stories can be so compelling. They aren't just roadmaps to success, they include information about the pitfalls you might come up against too. It all makes for interesting reading, and it's not like you have to do it all at once. You can start out small by finding the time to read a couple of pages every day. Once you start getting into their stories, you'll be inspired to read some more. Before you know it, you'll have read a bunch of really good books and learned a lot. Trust me, once you get started, it won't feel like homework or studying."

I tried to look thoughtful, but I was actually thinking about my schedule. It was already really tight and I wasn't sure I'd be able to find any extra time to read. Again, I felt Granddaddy surveying me.

"Look around at your classmates and think about the amount of work they do. In one sense, you're all equal... you're all expected to do the same amount of work. All that ordinary knowledge is helping you build an ordinary foundation for your future. Some of your classmates will settle for what they get taught in the classroom and try to build their future with that. They'll do an ordinary amount of work and be satisfied with their ordinary future. If they want more... if you want more, then you have to understand that it will require more effort on your part.

"Extraordinary futures are the result of extraordinary effort. Every extra minute you utilize today is helping you build your future. You're the one who gets to decide how many extra minutes are needed. You're the one who gets to decide how extraordinary you want your life to be. Every extra minute you apply strengthens your Kaizen."

Granddaddy had stopped talking and was probably waiting for me to say something, but I still didn't have anything to say. I wasn't ready to commit to doing more work. I wanted to know what the heck a kaizen was, but Granddaddy started talking before I could ask him.

"Come to think of it, maybe one of the biggest advantages the Romans... or the Egyptians, for that matter... had was that they didn't have smart phones."

"What?" I asked, totally thrown off by his comment.

"I get so annoyed when people say aliens built the pyramids. It seems to me that aliens with enough technology to travel through space would have had the technology to build the pyramids much quicker. The people who lived back then were absolutely capable of building them. Their lives were very different from ours too. One of their greatest resources might have been time. They had the people, the raw materials, and no smart phones or video games. They had the time to build the pyramids."

The movie *Gladiator* popped into my mind, and I chuckled at the thought of Russell Crowe dressed as a gladiator checking his text messages.

"If you were to add it all up, how much time do you think you've spent playing video games?"

I shrugged. I honestly didn't know. I'd never thought about it. "Listen, I'm not trying to give you a hard time about how you're spending your time. You're doing a great job. But when it comes to finding the time, the only way to find it is to believe it can be found. You won't find any time at all if you decide there aren't any extra minutes in your day before you even start looking."

"You're right. I know I can probably find a couple of minutes a day. You know, Granddaddy, I really like hearing all this stuff..." I paused.

"But?" Granddaddy asked and then waited.

"But... I almost feel like I'm not doing enough now. When we started talking, I was feeling pretty good about things... I guess what I really want to ask is... will it ever be enough? I don't want that ordinary life. I want more than that. But, man, I've got a pretty full schedule."

Granddaddy smiled. "Here's the thing. It doesn't matter what I think. It only matters what you think. Every journey comes with hurdles and struggles, but that doesn't mean you have to suffer through the process. And right now, it sounds a little bit like you're thinking you have to suffer by giving something up so you can keep moving forward. Think about your workouts. How do you feel at the end of a workout?"

"I feel great. Glad it's over, but stronger. I feel like I've accomplished something and I'm ready for... I don't know, for whatever."

"Exactly. It was work, hard work, but you do it anyway. You work out because you know it's going to help you. Did you feel that way after the first time you worked out?"

"Oh man, that first time just about killed me."

Granddaddy laughed. "I can believe it. I bet it took you a few weeks to get into the flow of working out too."

"Yeah, it did. But once I got going it was nothing. I had a plan and I knew what to do. It was easy, really." Then I smiled at

Granddaddy nodding my head. "Ohhhh, I get it."

Granddaddy nodded his head approvingly. "Exactly. Once you got started, it got easier. What matters most is how you feel about your efforts. If you find yourself suffering through the process without experiencing any kind of gain, that's when you want to stop and take a closer look at what you're doing. Don't be afraid of the work ahead of you. Focus your attention on the work in front of you. Focus on building your Kaizen."

THE MARSHMALLOW TEST

*"Good, better, best; never let it rest till your good
is better and your better is best."*
—Unknown Author

This time I spoke before Granddaddy could continue.

"What the heck is a Kaizen?"

"Well, Dakota, it's another secret I learned during World War II." "Did you learn it from Colonel Reynolds?" I asked.

"I learned a lot of great lessons from Colonel Reynolds and General Eisenhower, aka Ike, while we were fighting Hitler. I learned things that kept me alive during the war, and things that helped me come home filled with knowledge, wisdom, and insight as a result. Thanks to them, and all the other great men I served with, I can proudly say I'm a part of what journalist Dan Rather called *The Greatest Generation*. We were the generation that survived the Great Depression. We won World War II and then we came home and worked on building the United States of America."

The pride in his voice came through his words, but he looked sad. "It's strange. Back then, people said the whole name... The United States of America. It was like it meant more back then. Now, people don't say it like that. Now they just say USA."

I could tell he felt bad about that. "I wish I could be a part of something like that... part of a Greatest Generation."

"You have different opportunities ahead of you. And that's a good thing. It's one thing to have everybody on the same page and working together when it comes to fighting a war. If you aren't, bad things happen. But when the fighting's done, we need to follow our own talents and dreams, and you were asking about Kaizen."

I perked up. "So what is it?"

"Well, there's a bit of a story that goes along with it. Like I said, I learned a lot about life while serving in the military, but there were other military leaders I learned from that I never met or had the privilege of serving under. To tell you about Kaizen, I have to tell you about them. There's also the marshmallow test to consider," Granddaddy said and gave me an appraising look. "Are you up to it?"

"A marshmallow test? Seriously? I would hope I'd be up to a marshmallow test. How hard can it be if that's what it's called?"

"I guess we'll find out. Right now, in order for you to truly understand the secret of Kaizen, you need more background information. Let me see," Granddaddy said peering at me. "Where do I start? I guess we need to talk a little bit more about World War II.

"Initially, the United States wanted no part of what was going on in Europe. Hitler knew we were still suffering from the effects of the Great Depression and had determined it would take the United States a full two years to produce and transport a fully equipped and fully trained fighting force all the way to

Europe. But Japan bombed us at Pearl Harbor, and with Winston Churchill's urging, President Roosevelt finally decided to take this country to war and declared the United States an 'Arsenal of Democracy' against both Hitler and Japan."

Granddaddy nodded his head like he agreed with President Roosevelt. "It was a bold move, but it left our country with a huge challenge. Roosevelt, with some help from Churchill, had decided that we needed to defeat Hitler first. Most of our resources were being dedicated to defeating Hitler anyway. But now we were sending our men to fight—in opposite directions! Hitler was probably pretty happy when he heard that. Now that the United States was going in two different directions, he figured that by the time we could get our military forces over to Europe, he would have already won the war. And he might have been right except for one thing. Any chance you might know what I'm talking about?"

I was listening to every word he was saying, but I didn't have a clue what he was talking about. I shook my head hoping he would keep going.

Granddaddy shrugged. "I had a feeling you wouldn't. But only because it isn't in a lot of history books... at least not as much as it should be. The reason we were able to pull off the impossible was because the women of this country stepped in and took over the work of the men so the men could go and fight. Our women worked in automobile factories that had been turned into war factories, 24 hours a day, 7 days a week, 365 days a year."

"Women?" I asked, surprise evident in my voice. "Really? I thought you were going to say it was some kind of secret weapon no one knew about."

Granddaddy looked at me. "Well, they were kind of a secret weapon. Hitler certainly didn't take them into account. He underestimated our resolve, and our women. Our women helped put our men in a position to be on European soil, fully equipped, fully armed, and ready to fight in less than six months while simultaneously equipping another set of troops to fight in Asia against Japan after Pearl Harbor."

"Wow! That's impressive," I said. "I never realized women played such a big role in World War II."

"Most people don't know. Again, it's not a fact that's in your history books. People also don't know how many lives were lost in war factory accidents. We lost more women in the factories than we did soldiers during the first six months of the war."

I was stunned by this information. "In all the old war movies I've ever seen, all the women do is serve coffee, dance, sing, or be nurses. I don't get it. War movies always seem to be about how brave the men are. Why didn't they show what the women were doing too? Why didn't they show it like it really was?"

"The answer is complicated. With the black and white war movies, they did it that way because people needed to keep their morale up. People didn't need to be reminded of the price they were paying for being at war. They were surrounded by it every day, so the movies were made with happy endings. They romanticized them as a way of keeping hope alive.

"As times changed, movies started showing more drama because film makers felt like the government wasn't telling the public everything that was going on. So those movies showed more about the tragedies of war. They were still focusing on the glory of the fight, and the bravery of our men, but the endings weren't always happy.

"It's only recently that we've started seeing women get recognized as soldiers in movies. It's really sad that all the women who worked tirelessly to support our victories have never really been represented or recognized for the depth of their contribution in those World War II movies—or at any other time in history."

"It doesn't seem very fair."

"You're right. It isn't fair, but that's one of the things that happens with war. Everybody pays a price. It doesn't matter which side you're on, either. The men and women of every country involved with World War II did what they had to do to keep going, to keep hope alive. I'm truly grateful for all the support we got from home during those hard times. Even for those silly romantic war movies.

But let's get back on track. Now where did I leave off?"

"Kaizen?" I offered hopefully.

"Not yet. We're still leading up to that... and the marshmallow test." Granddaddy smiled. "Can't forget about that." I shook my head, but Granddaddy ignored it.

"Okay... We were at war on two fronts. The Japanese war machine did a number on us at Pearl Harbor and needed to be stopped if this country was going to survive. That job fell heavily on the shoulders of one man. With most of our country's resources battling Hitler in Europe, he was faced with the task of defeating the Japanese in Asia with only the bare minimum of soldiers and supplies. This American's name was General Douglas MacArthur, the son of the great American General Arthur MacArthur. This amazing father-son team is the only fa-ther-son team in the history of the United States to be awarded with the Medal of Honor while both were still alive. You know this Kaizen secret you're so eager to learn?"

"Yeah?" I responded with guarded enthusiasm.

"I learned Kaizen because of General Douglas MacArthur. But listen carefully... I've never met this American legend. This is just another example of the magical power of books!"

"I've never met him either," I joked. "But I do remember the name MacArthur from my history books. I'm pretty sure there wasn't anything about Kaizen, though. I think I'd have remembered that."

"I'm pretty sure they didn't mention Kaizen in your history books too. Any chance you remember anything else you learned about MacArthur?"

I started wracking my brain and remembered a picture of a general with a pipe. Then I remembered something else and blurted it out. "President Truman fired MacArthur during the Korean war.

Is that right?"

Granddaddy looked at me, shook his head a little, and then continued. "Yes, that's correct, but that was just a headline. Macarthur was a brilliant military leader and did a lot more than get fired by Truman. He fought in World War I, World War II, and the Korean War. In 1944, he became one of only five men in the history of the United States to rise to rank of General of the Army. MacArthur had commanded our Pacific forces against Japan, and when the war was over, he was ap-pointed Supreme Commander of the Allied Forces in Japan."

Some of the things Granddaddy was saying started jogging my memory. "Now that you mention it, I do remember studying some of that stuff. Didn't he rule Japan?"

"Yes and no. He definitely had a tremendous effect on the country after the war. He helped Japan create a democratic constitution that's named after him and is still in use today. He broke up Japan's big companies, like Roosevelt had done with the huge companies and corporations that were starting to monopolize our economic landscape. MacArthur helped Japan start labor unions. He helped them rebuild their country and get back on track so they could compete with the rest of the World's industrial powers."

"It's really weird hearing you talk about this. I remember studying parts of it now. It's different hearing you talk about it because it sounds real now. I remember some dates too. I remember December 7th, 1941. That was the day they bombed Pearl Harbor. And I remember May 8th, 1945. That's the day the war was over. I remember the dates because I got tested on them. But now... I don't know... it's weird hearing you talk about people who were there. You were there."

I looked at Granddaddy but it was hard to imagine him suited up as a soldier. He was Granddaddy, but he had also been one of those men—like the ones in the pictures in my history book.

"You're right. I was there. But I'm here now, right where I want to be. I wanted to tell you about MacArthur because if it weren't for him, we probably wouldn't be talking about Kaizen at all. He didn't create it, but he was indirectly responsible for its application. Like I said, after World War II, MacArthur was put in charge of helping a war-torn Japan repair itself. But he was doing it without cell phones. There was no Internet, no email. He couldn't even count on being able to complete a regular old-fashioned phone call. I bet you can't even imagine that."

I nodded. He was right about that.

"MacArthur had to work with the people around him, utilizing the resources he had. One of the things he did that was really smart was to talk Dr. William Edwards Deming in to coming to Japan to help. Deming was an American who had been raised on his Grandfather's chicken farm in Iowa. He loved math and had earned PhDs from Yale University in mathematics and physics. He was a very smart and capable man, and when these two great minds got together, that was when the concept of Kaizen started taking root.

Not here in the United States of America, but in war-torn Japan."

"Did they make it up?"

"Yes and no. They didn't create the concept itself. The idea has been around for a while. Deming had been trying to get people in this country to work with the idea for years, but people weren't interested. It got the name Kaizen in Japan."

I was trying to stay focused, but I was getting frustrated. "Is there a reason why you aren't telling me what it is? Do you think I won't understand? Can't you just tell me what Kaizen is?"

"Can I tell you about the marshmallow test first?"

"Sure... Whatever," I sighed and turned to look at him. "Look. I'm sorry. You know I want to hear all of this. It just seems like there's a reason you aren't telling me what Kaizen is. If there's a test I have to take, can't I take it so we can be done with it and move on?" "There's only one question." "Ask," I said.

Granddaddy looked back at me. "If I tell you about Kaizen first, you might not understand it as well as you would if you were to hear about the marshmallow test first. Of course to hear about the marshmallow test means waiting to hear about Kaizen. So the question is, are you willing to hear about the marshmallow test first if it will help you understand Kaizen better?"

"And then you'll tell me about Kaizen after that?"

"Yes."

"Then bring on the marshmallow test."

Granddaddy rewarded my answer with a big smile. "Marshmallow tests have been around for a while now. The research started at Stanford University in the late 60s and early 70s with a group of psychologists trying to decide how old kids were when they started to develop the ability to wait for something they wanted. In other words, they wanted to know if these kids could delay gratification. The results were so interesting that other researchers focused right in on the interesting part and did their own marshmallow tests.

"They would have a kid between the ages of four and six sit at a table. On the table was a plate with one marshmallow on it. The researcher explained to the kid that he or she could eat the marshmallow right now, or, he or she could wait 15 minutes and then get another marshmallow. If the kid ate the marshmallow now, he or she would still have to wait the 15 minutes but wouldn't get another marshmallow. The researcher then left the room for

15 minutes."

"Really? That's the marshmallow test?"

"I know. It sounds really simple, Dakota, but this is what they found out. When they checked in on the kids who were given the test years later, the kids who had waited 15 minutes to get the extra marshmallow turned out to be more successful and appeared to be happier with their lives."

"So let me get this straight. You've been giving me a marshmallow test?" I said trying not to sound as annoyed as I was feeling.

Granddaddy shrugged. "The answer is yes. But I wasn't doing it because I wanted to know if you'd be willing to wait. I wanted *you* to be aware of the choice you made." I stared at him.

"The marshmallow test is interesting. And maybe there is a link between success and our ability to wait for a greater reward. But I think there's more to it than that. I think anybody is capable of waiting if they have the right goal in front of them. After all, if you don't have a goal or a good reason to wait, then why bother? Why bother with the step-by-step work if the goal it's leading to isn't meaningful to you?

"Sadly, that's the way it is for a lot of people. They do the work, but they don't care about the goal because it isn't their goal—it's someone else's goal. Why work harder if there's nothing in it for them? Instead, they say "the heck with this" and move on to something else. Think about your teammates. I bet you have a few teammates who play sports just because they can. Think about your classmates. How many of them have jobs? How long do they keep them? You're the same age as they are and you have two jobs, *and* you study, *and* you work out, *and* you play two sports."

I could feel myself starting to puff up a little again.

"When it comes to the kids who ate the marshmallow, and by the way, two-thirds of them ate it, why did they eat it? What if they'd just had lunch and weren't hungry enough to be interested in waiting 15 minutes? What if they didn't really like marshmallows enough to wait 15 minutes for another one? Maybe they ate the one in front of them because they were kids. Is it okay to use a marshmallow as an indicator of future success? How would you feel if someone asked you one question and then told you your future based on one single answer?"

"I wouldn't like it."

"No one would. Especially if their one question was the wrong question. The researchers had their goal, but did it have anything to do with the kid's goal? We do our best work when we have goals that are meaningful to us. That's why goals are so important. That's why I knew you could pass the marshmallow test. You have goals. You know that sometimes you have to get through one door before you can get to the next door. Not everyone understands that. And then when they do set goals, they make the mistake of choosing goals they don't have any control over. For example, what would happen if you set a goal of winning a football game?"

"That's not a good idea," I said. "I can't decide our team is going to win a game. All I can do is prepare as best as I can and then put all my effort into everything I do. If we win, we win."

"Exactly!" Granddaddy beamed. "You can't plan for your team to win. Winning or losing is the result of the contest. The only thing you have control over is what you bring onto the field. I wish more kids had your kind of insight. But that's not really a fair thing to say, either. There are plenty of kids who wonder about all these things. I bet some of your old friends think about stuff like this too."

Granddaddy shook his head. "These are the kinds of things every kid should be learning. They need guidance so they can make better choices earlier in life. That's one of the things about Kaizen. There isn't an age limit to learning it. If the United States embraced Kaizen the way they do in Japan, you'd already be applying Kaizen to your life, and so would your classmates. Don't get me wrong. It wouldn't cure everything that's upside-down for kids, but it would be a good place to start."

"So I don't have a Kaizen yet?"

"You already apply many Kaizen principles in your life. You just don't know it. Are you ready to hear the secret of Kaizen?" "Bring it on."

KAIZEN

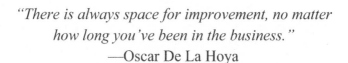

*"There is always space for improvement, no matter
how long you've been in the business."*
—Oscar De La Hoya

"The word Kaizen breaks down to Kai—which means change, and Zen—which means good. It literally means change is good, or change causes improvement. Other people say it means: self-changing for the best of all. The idea of Kaizen was already a part of the Japanese culture prior to the war. It wasn't until after the war that it became thought of as a constant and never-ending commitment to increasing the quality of Japanese businesses every single day.

"What's really interesting is that MacArthur originally brought Dr. Deming to Japan to help the Japanese prepare for their 1951 census. But because of his background in statistics and concepts of quality, Deming started lecturing to Japan's chief executives and the Union of Japanese Scientists and Engineers about how small improvements to the quality of a process could result in increased productivity and market share.

"This thinking helped Japan get back on its feet quicker after the War. By 1951, the Japanese thought so highly of Deming for his contributions to Japan's progress that they created an award in his name, *The Deming Prize*."

"That's cool. What do you have to do to win the prize?" I asked.

"It's awarded for contributions to the field of Total Quality Management. If you want I can give you more details," Granddaddy said with a smile.

I grimaced. "That's okay. I think I got the basics."

Granddaddy continued, "There was another interesting thing that happened as a result of Deming's influence. The US Air Force offered training to Japanese businessmen based on Deming's approach. One of the people who took part in the program was a man named Mr. Sakichi Toyoda. He was the founder of Toyota... yes, the car Toyota!"

"So Dr. Deming had something to do with Toyota too?"

"To some degree. I think the point here is that Japan had been devastated by WWII. They knew there was work to be done and they were willing to do it. What they needed was a process. Deming's ideas became embedded in their approach to rebuilding their industries, their economy, and their lives.

"People became personally invested in looking at what was in front of them and making sure that whatever they were producing was the best it could be. Everybody was a part of the process too. It wasn't just management's decision. It was the people standing in front of the machines too. They all worked together, each person committed to bringing the best of themselves to their work so the combined end product would also be a reflection of their best too."

"I may not be that old, but even I know people don't do that around here. There used to be a great pizza place down the block. We went there all the time, but then they hired this new guy and it wasn't the same. He didn't last long, but even after he left the pizza wasn't as good. I don't know... maybe that's not what you were talking about."

"Oh, but it is. It's exactly what I'm talking about. Japan really embraced the concept that everybody is part of the process—even the little guy making the pizza. They applied the idea that when everyone is a part of the process and brings their best to the job, the end result is the best product available. The result was that Japan became one of the most powerful economies in the world, second only to the United States. Not only that, Deming turned down all the royalties he could have earned for all the systems and products he invented while helping Japan become the top industrial power it is today."

"So that's Kaizen?" I asked a little confused.

"Yes, those are the basics of Kaizen."

"But I don't get it. I don't have a business. I don't work in a big company or anything like that. I have a couple of jobs, but they're simple jobs. I'm just a teenager. How does this relate to me?"

"Just a teenager?" Granddaddy asked. "Does that mean you aren't smart enough or old enough to start your own business? I understand how it might not sound like it has anything to do with you, but think about it for a minute. Think about the way people talk about kids your age. I hear what people say too. They think teenagers don't know how to commit to anything. They think you all give up before you try. They think you expect everybody to take care of you rather than stepping up and taking care of yourself. Is that how you see yourself?"

"No!" I shot back. "I can take care of myself. I've been doing it for years now."

Granddaddy nodded his head. "The sad part is that if the idea of Kaizen had been embraced by our country and in the way we raise our kids, you and your friends might already have a business going. The last part of the story with Dr. Deming is that when he tried to get people in the United States to employ his ideas, no one was really interested. It wasn't until the 1980s, when the United States started losing economic ground to the quality of Japanese products, that they finally started grasping the value of Deming's ideas."

Granddaddy looked at me. "You may not see a bunch of business opportunities in front of you, but that doesn't mean you can't employ Kaizen in your life right now. Like I said, you already are. Dr. Deming believed the philosophy and ethics of quality work and reducing waste would eventually give the Japanese the ability to dominate the markets of the world. He was right, but he also taught that quality was not just a matter of meeting certain standards. It was a living, breathing process of never-ending improvement."

I looked out at the rain, trying to wrap my brain around what he was saying. Granddaddy must have read the expression on my face.

"Let me repeat that last sentence again, Dakota. Dr. Deming taught that quality was not just a matter of meeting certain standards, but rather was a living, breathing process of never-ending improvement. In short, he wasn't just talking about business, he was talking about a way of life too. Can you see how that might relate to you and all your fellow teenagers?"

"Um... maybe. You're saying that I can use Kaizen in my life right now? That I don't have to be in business to use it?" I looked at him hopefully.

"Yes, that's exactly what I'm saying."

I was glad I got the answer right, but I didn't really understand what he was talking about. "I've never heard of anything like this before. It sounds like a good idea, but if it really is good, then how come I've never heard of it before?"

Granddaddy sighed. "One reason is really silly and definitely sad, but it's true. We don't have an English translation for the word Kaizen. We have no word in our entire language that stresses small, continuous, never-ending improvement. People can be close minded too, and after the war they might have heard the word Kaizen, but there was very little chance of people in this country employing a concept that even remotely sounded like it had anything to do with the Japanese."

"Huh. That's the reason?"

"There are lots of reasons," Granddaddy said. "We had our own focus here. We didn't suffer the extensive structural damages they experienced in Europe and Asia, and our country had already proved it was capable of rebuilding after tough times. This was just another tough time for us, so we employed the same practices we had employed all along. We didn't feel like we needed something like Kaizen. We were all working towards the *American Dream*."

"Now that, I've heard of."

"I'm sure. That's one of the things I was fighting for when I was in Europe. We all did our part so we could come home and claim our part of the American Dream. I'm curious. What do you think the American Dream is?"

I shrugged. "I don't know. Like maybe owning my own house and having my own business and being able to retire early so I can do whatever I want to?"

"That's pretty much what most people think the American Dream is. Maybe that's why so many people can't seem to achieve it." "What do you mean?" I asked.

"Well, those are good things, but it's hard to imagine a home and a business would be everybody's idea of a happy and successful life. Maybe that's one of the big differences between the American Dream and Kaizen. With the American Dream, we're taught to invest in our long-term future. With Kaizen, it's about investing in our everyday life."

I thought about that for a minute. "Doesn't Anthony Robbins say something about constant improvement?"

"He does," Granddaddy said. "He created the acronym C.A.N.I. The letters stand for *Constant and Never-Ending Improvement*. Robbins believes that if there is a chance of obtaining true security in this world, then it comes from knowing that every single day you are improving your life in some way. Through CANI, you're always growing, making yourself more capable, and bringing your honest and best self to whatever you're doing. When this becomes a way of living, you become a welcome addition to your family, friends, community, and workplace. Robbins said that this commitment is the only true sense of security a human being can know."

"What does that mean... the only security you can know?"

"Well, we were just talking about the American Dream, but if you think about it, there's no guarantee everyone's going to get it. A lot of people will get there, but will they be secure when they do? Do you know what a foreclosure is?" I nodded.

"There are plenty of people who achieved their dream of owning a home but then couldn't afford it and ended up losing it. They lost the security of having a home. I think what Robbins means is that the things we can truly feel secure about are the things we carry with us through life. When you commit to something like CANI or Kaizen, your sense of security isn't determined by the things you collect or by what goes on around you. Your true security is in knowing you are always striving to be your best self and to bring your best self to the situation, no matter what you're doing... even if it's just making a pizza."

"I do like pizza," I said with a smile.

"There are a lot of other people who believe in this path too. Helen Keller believed security is a superstition. She said, 'Life is either a daring adventure or it's nothing.' She had some serious handicaps to work with and yet she didn't back down and let others do her work. She got out there anyway.

"Sometimes it's hard for people to see life like that, though. They don't feel strong enough or they're just plain afraid. It's easier for them to go home, lock the doors and windows, and pull the shades tight. All they have to do is watch a little TV or read the newspaper to have their belief that home is the safest place verified."

"That's sad," I said. "First of all, it isn't always safer inside. Maybe it is compared to being outside... I'm just saying. But I get how it's like we've become prisoners, only instead of having someone lock us up, we lock ourselves up."

Granddaddy nodded. "I like to think the people in our country will come to understand there are other ways to reach for success and security. There are definitely people working on providing more opportunities for hearing about it. There are researchers, psychologists, life and success coaches, and others who have embraced the concepts of Kaizen and CANI who are always analyzing and dissecting success.

"They know success leaves clues. They know Kaizen and CANI are a part of it. They want us to know it too. We've already improved on our understanding of it by developing a new acronym—CANDI. It stands for *Constant and Never-ending* **Deliberate** *Improvement*. The thought here is to stop shooting blindly for improvement. Deliberately, scientifically, and systematically pursue excellence by constantly improving on things that have already been proven to bring success."

"I like that they added the word deliberate," I said. "It gets right to the point that it doesn't just happen, we have to do it. I think that's the big problem. People are too lazy to do things."

"Some people are, but a lot of people are afraid. They don't know how to take action because nobody has ever taken the time to explain it to them. Think about it this way. You started with a book. You had coaches who recognized the potential in you and worked with you and encouraged you. Would you be where you are right now if those things hadn't happened?"

I shrugged. I didn't want to think about what my life might have been like. Would I have ended up like my brother?

Granddaddy shook his head. "I don't know the answer either. What I do know is that even with those advantages, your success is still the result of your decision to show up and do the work—even when it's not a whole lot of fun. But how great does it feel when you put your sincere and honest effort into the things you do because you've committed to a path of improvement?"

"Gotta admit. It feels really good." I turned and looked at Granddaddy completely surprised by what I had just realized. "And no one can take it away from me. Not now, not ever."

NEW FRIENDS FROM THE PAST

"There is more treasure in books than in all the pirates' loot on Treasure Island." —Walt Disney

I expected Granddaddy to respond to what I'd said, but he was quiet now too, almost like he was giving me time to think about it. I had to admit, it felt good—almost powerful. Not in a "go out and take on the world" kind of way. It was more like knowing that I probably really could do whatever I put my mind to. That's what I'd been doing so far. I'd just never thought of it like that before.

In sports, there's always someone trying to do the same thing you are—win. But that wasn't what I was feeling now. Right now it was more like I understood that everything I had accomplished up until now was totally because I had done the work. No one had done it for me. No one had forced me to do it. I didn't hit the snooze button on my alarm clock. I got up, and I put everything I had into the work ahead of me. Just the thought of all that I had accomplished so far blew my mind because now, when I looked back at what I'd done, it almost looked easy.

To be honest, it really hadn't been that hard to work out. I liked it. It was easy practicing because I liked being prepared to compete. Up until this minute, though, I'd thought it had been a struggle. Yes, some days were tougher than others, but for the most part it was always easy because I was doing it for a reason. It felt even better realizing I wasn't doing it just to be prepared in case I needed to defend myself against Pops. Now I was doing it because it felt good to push myself to achieve more. I could now see how each success inspired me to push a little harder. I shook my head in disbelief.

"Why are you shaking your head, Dakota?" Granddaddy asked.

I shrugged my shoulders again. "I don't know. It's weird to think about this stuff. I've never thought about myself like this... like there was anything more. I know I'm old enough for a lot of things, but I've never thought about myself as anything other than a kid in high school just doing time until I could get out on my own. The stuff you're talking about makes me wonder if I'm more than that."

"Good... because you are more than just a kid in high school. The truth is, you and all your classmates are more than that. You're all very close to being adults and going out into the world. I wish your classmates had some of the same drive and determination you have."

"But wouldn't that get in the way? If we all wanted the same things, wouldn't that be a problem?"

"If you all wanted the exact same thing it might be, but it doesn't happen like that in the real world. We all want different things because we all have different likes and dislikes."

I looked at Granddaddy. "How did you know what you wanted?"

"I didn't at first. I knew I wanted to get out of the house and I decided to enlist, but I didn't have any idea after that. It was when I started listening to Colonel Reynolds that I began to think about other things. Even then I didn't come back with a clear path in mind. I wasn't anywhere near as focused as you are."

"So how'd you do it? How'd you get where you are now?" I asked, realizing I still didn't know much about Granddaddy, what he did, or how he'd become successful.

"Friends and mentors."

I thought about that for a few seconds and then stared at the ground. I didn't really have a lot of friends, and I didn't know anyone besides Granddaddy and my coaches who said anything worth listening to.

"When I was your age," Granddaddy continued, "I didn't have a lot of friends. Not only that, I was so determined to enlist, I didn't tell anyone about my plans. I didn't trust anyone enough to talk about my ideas or dreams."

I understood that feeling.

"After the war, I had a lot of questions and no one to ask. I wasn't serving under Colonel Reynolds anymore and I didn't know what to do next. It was a hard time because I felt very much like I had started something I might never be able to finish."

"What'd you do?" I asked, totally surprised at the thought of Granddaddy being unsure of himself.

He stared out into the storm. "One day I was walking, and I remembered something Colonel Reynolds had said. He told me to look at the new recruit on my right and the new recruit on my left, and then he asked me if I knew what the difference between us would be in ten years."

Granddaddy leaned towards me conspiratorially.

"Fortunately he didn't wait for me to answer because I didn't have a clue what the answer was! He explained that the difference between us as the teenagers we were now, and the men we would be in ten years, would be the books we had read and the people we chose to spend our time with. Of course, like a lot of the things he said to me, it took me a while to understand and apply his words of wisdom.

"Then, one day I walked into a bookstore, picked up a book, and started reading. I don't even remember what the book was. I just opened it up to the middle and started reading and it was like listening to Colonel Reynolds all over again. I was so grateful for that first book. So grateful I had remembered what Colonel Reynolds had said. When I started reading, I didn't feel so alone anymore. I felt like I was having a conversation with someone I would have been friends with if we'd been able to meet in person."

"You didn't get to meet the guy who'd written the book? Did you try?"

Granddaddy chuckled. "No. That wasn't possible. He'd been dead for a very long time."

"You don't remember who he was?"

"Not anymore. I've read so many books since then that I can't remember who the first author was. Ever since that first book, though, I've grown to think of each author as a friend. Each of them did one of the most meaningful things a friend can do. They cared so much about me that they shared their knowledge and wisdom for living a long, meaningful, purposeful, and happy life. They became my role models. What's even more interesting is that some of them became role models for things I decided I didn't want."

"What?"

"Well, just because someone's written a book, that doesn't mean you're going to agree with what they say. When I disagree with what they've written, I try to understand it from their point of view. In life, it isn't enough to say you disagree with what someone says. It won't carry any weight until you can explain how what you think is different from what they think. It would be like someone telling you he didn't like your wrestling technique but couldn't tell you why or what he thinks you should be doing instead."

I nodded my head.

"I didn't dismiss what an author said just because I disagreed. In fact, it was when I disagreed with what they were saying that I sometimes was finally able to really make sense of what I believed. So I gave them the same respect friends give each other. I respected the argument and chalked it up to an agreement to disagree."

I chuckled. "My girlfriend... I mean Jenn, says that sometimes." I mimicked her voice as best as I could. "'We'll just have to agree to disagree with this one.'"

Granddaddy laughed. "What do you think would happen if you didn't? If you didn't let it go and kept trying to make your point?"

"We'd probably get into a fight... unless one of us backed down."

"That's another great thing about all my author friends. They don't fight me or bully me into agreeing with them. They give me time to contemplate and think about what they've said. And, they're always ready to continue the conversation when I'm ready to read more."

I shook my head, but with a big smile on my face.

"You're so cool sometimes. I've never met anyone who'd admit to having a bunch of dead friends."

"Maybe not, but they were my first role models after the war. I have a lot of living friends too, and believe it or not, they feel the same way about their book role models too. It's one thing we have in common. We understand that knowledge is a dead end unless it's shared."

"Okay, so who's one of your favorite dead friends? Who did you learn something from that really impressed you?"

"All of them pretty much had at least one interesting thing to say, but there are a few who come to mind. First of all, I want to be clear that I'm not talking about reading text books like your history book. That's a great starting point, but I'm talking about people whose lives have been captured in words so that they can be shared with people interested in finding out more. Some stories have been chronicled by other people. Some are autobiographies. All of them have knowledge and wisdom to share. When I think back, one of the most interesting people I've ever read was about

Socrates."

"We were talking about him earlier, right?"

"Yes. As I said, he was a Greek philosopher who was always asking questions. He believed we already have all the answers inside of us. We just need to ask or hear better questions to get us looking in the right places."

"That's kind of like what you were saying about reading books and being able to explain why we agree or disagree with what they are saying?"

"Well said!" Granddaddy exclaimed, his look, one of approval. "When I read about Socrates, I understood what he meant. Don't ever let anyone stop you from asking questions. I also decided it was probably smarter to ask some of those questions inside my own head first, or to do some research before asking someone else out loud. If you remember that, you won't fear situations where you don't immediately know the answer. You will grow to welcome your questions because the more questions you ask, the more your life will expand."

"I can see how asking the wrong person might not be a good idea. You wouldn't want to ask a jailer how to pick a lock." "That's an interesting analogy. What made you think of it?" "Didn't Socrates go to jail?" I asked, hoping I got it right.

"Socrates did get in a lot of trouble. Things were very different back then. Going against society or the rulers back then was pretty much a death sentence. Emperors and rulers saw death as the best deterrent for people who spoke out or physically rebelled against their rules. Socrates committed the crime of asking too many questions about why things were the way they were. Everybody kept expecting him to be put to death because he was doing it boldly and without fear of the consequences. The government was nervous about executing him because so many people were listening to him. Instead, they told him they'd spare his life if he would just stop asking questions. Can you guess what happened?"

I knew the answer to this one too because it had blown me away when I read it. "He drank the hemlock on purpose."

"He sure did. He said, 'An unexamined life wasn't worth living.' How ironic is it that Greece, famous for its democracy, tried to get Socrates to stop asking questions because they were worried more people would start asking questions too. And hey, I know this goes without saying, but remember that what Socrates did was powerful during his lifetime. It's not a good solution for someone living during our lifetime. Our job is to contribute as much as we can to life. You can't contribute anything if you're six feet underground. A better way to honor Socrates is to keep asking questions. 'Know thyself,' as he would say."

"I will," I said firmly.

"Want to know what I learned from my old friend Hitler?" Granddaddy asked.

I looked at Granddaddy in complete disbelief. "I can't believe that you would call Hitler an old friend!"

"I figured that might be a tough one to understand. It was tough for me to accept that he had something to teach me too... at first. But regardless of the personal impressions of him I developed during the war, despite the fact that I could never relate to his ideology or his methodology, I still learned from him."

"What could you possibly learn from him?" I said, trying to wrap my brain around the fact that Granddaddy had just called

Hitler a friend. "He was a butcher!"

It was the first time since we'd started talking that I was actually nervous about what he was going to say next. Hitler was a monster. Everyone knew it too. I stared at him, daring him to challenge what I'd said about Hitler.

"He taught all of us that power can corrupt the hearts and minds of the people who wield it, and that absolute power corrupts absolutely!"

I'd heard something like that before. I'd probably read it in my history book. "But everybody said that. How can you say you learned it from Hitler if everybody says it?"

Granddaddy smiled. "Sometimes it takes really big events for us to learn really big lessons. Just because millions of people learned it all together doesn't mean it isn't worth learning. It was a very hard lesson to learn too, but we know it now. There was another lesson in there that isn't quite as clear until you start thinking about it.

"Change isn't limited to the circle you draw around yourself while you pursue your dreams. It's like those circular waves emanating from a pebble tossed in a pond. Change has the power to influence and affect other people's lives too. What I learned from Hitler is to always consider who might be on the results end of the actions I take. When the results of change are likely to hurt or harm, or show no respect or consideration for life, it's probably worth more thought before taking action."

I was quiet while I thought about what Granddaddy had said. It floored me that he was able to so easily create a lesson out of Hitler, and I couldn't help but wonder how many friends I would find in the books I was now determined to read. What would I learn?

I looked at Granddaddy. He had an air about him that commanded my respect. Not out of fear, though. I genuinely respected him and what he was sharing with me. It gave me chills. I wondered if I'd be like him when I was his age. I couldn't wait for my adventure to begin and that was what this felt like—a new adventure. This day really was changing things. I decided right then and there I was going to start reading books and start talking to people.

WHEN THE STUDENT IS READY,
THE MASTER WILL APPEAR

"A student of life considers the world a classroom."
—Harvey Mackay

"It might not be fair to stop with mentioning just those two old friends. I've learned so many important lessons over the years. Jesus taught me to look within myself to find the Kingdom of Heaven. Buddha taught me about Enlightenment, Nirvana, and how to be happy with what I have instead of worrying about what I don't have. There's King Solomon, Muhammad the Prophet, and Martin Luther King, Jr.," Granddaddy grinned. "The list is quite a bit longer, but I'm sure you don't want to sit here while I go through it."

"It's kind of interesting. I've heard of most of the names you've talked about today. I just never realized they were interesting before." "Dakota, you know who Gandhi was, right?" I nodded my head.

"When I first started reading I came across something he said that really stuck with me. Gandhi said we should live as if we were going to die tomorrow, and learn as if we were going to live forever." I nodded and tried to look thoughtful.

"Maybe you understand what that means, but I sure didn't when I read it. I think I understand it now. I talked earlier about being aware of the ripples we make with our actions. A lot of people will take the time to stop and try to predict the consequences of their actions so that they don't miss anything and end up accidentally causing damage. It's kind of a 'look before you leap' strategy.

"Unfortunately, people can get so stuck worrying about the consequences that they never take action. That's what people are referring to when they say things like 'Don't put off until tomorrow what you can do today' or 'Live your life to the fullest' or 'There's no time like the present.' Each one of those phrases is in line with what Gandhi said. They are all reminders that even though we can live long lives, we experience our life one moment at a time. If we don't live that moment, the opportunity to live it is lost."

"That explains it better. It makes me think about keeping my eye on the ball. I mean... when you're on the football field, and you get the ball, there's already a plan in place. But you still have to look around to make sure it's going to work. If you can see it isn't, then you have to adjust the plan by figuring out what you can do to get yourself in a better position. Either way, you still have to go for it. Actually, it works pretty much the same way with wrestling too. The only difference is that wrestling is man against man and football is team against team."

"What do you think the second part means, the part about learning like you're going to live forever?"

"I'm not sure about that. It sounds a little bit like doing homework for the rest of your life."

Granddaddy laughed. "I can't disagree. It does sound like that, and that's probably why most people quit learning after they get out of school. They feel like their head is full of enough knowledge for them to get the stuff they want. What do you think? Will that strategy work for you? Will your high school education or your college education be enough to get you where you want to go?"

"I'm not sure. If you'd asked me that when we sat down, I might have said yes, but right now, I'm not sure... I like what you said about reading. Is that what you mean by learning?"

"That's part of it. Think of it like this. Say you really, really wanted to learn how to do something like sky diving, but you kept putting it off because you couldn't seem to find the time, or because it made you too nervous when you thought about taking that first step out of a plane. Every year on your birthday, you remember how much you want to learn how to jump, but each birthday passes without you doing anything about it. Then, one day, you're 76 years old—like I am today—and you realize you're never going to jump. How do think you'd feel? Oh... and don't forget... if you'd taken the time to learn it when you were 20 years old and first thought about it, you would have jumped at least 56 jumps by the time you're 76."

"Is that something you'd wished you'd done?" I asked.

"It's something I did."

I looked at him with amazement. "Wait... Does that mean you jumped out of an airplane today?"

"No... Not today. I jumped yesterday so I could be here with you today."

"Did you learn how to do it in the Army?"

"Nope. I wanted to do it, so I figured out how to make it happen."

"You've jumped 56 times?" I could feel my voice getting louder but I couldn't believe what I was hearing.

"Actually, as of yesterday, I've jumped 93 times. But don't lose track of the point here. If I'd given up on the idea of learning something new after quitting high school and enlisting, I probably wouldn't have made any jumps. If everybody settled for what they learned in school, we probably wouldn't have computers yet, or electric cars, or laser eye surgery, or CAT scans. Our world continues to progress because people continue to pursue knowledge.

"Not only that, but because people continue to challenge themselves to learn and grow, when they hit 76 years old, they can look back at what they've accomplished and feel good about the contributions they've made. They probably won't stop there either because they'll be too excited about where the things they learn today will lead them tomorrow."

I hesitated, but then my question came out in a rush. "Do you think I'll ever do something important?" "Absolutely," Granddaddy said without hesitation.

I smiled, but I was looking at the floor. "Like what?"

"Dakota, I can't predict exactly what you're going to do. You get to make that decision. But I can tell you one thing I think you'll be really good at."

"What?" I asked, excited to hear what spectacular thing Granddaddy thought I would do.

"I think you're going to make a great coach one day." "Oh," I said, looking back down at the floor.

"What's wrong with being a coach?" Granddaddy asked.

"Nothing... I guess... I just thought maybe you'd see me doing something more important."

"You'll do a lot of meaningful and important things. I don't have any doubt about that, either. But I also believe that as you get older and start experiencing success, you'll remember what it was like being a teenager, and you'll think a lot about the people who helped guide you. There isn't a day of my life that goes by without me thinking about Colonel Reynolds. You've already had great people in your life helping you. Your coaches, Tony Robbins, and now you're going to be reading about other people who will be coaching you with their knowledge and wisdom too. Sharing what you've learned along the way is like a rite of passage. Trust me, you'll have a burning desire to do it, and you'll be great at it."

I nodded, but it didn't sound all that exciting. I wanted him to tell me he thought I'd be an Olympic champion, or a millionaire, or something like that.

Granddaddy continued, "Have I told you that I wrestled in high school too?"

"No," I said, surprised. "You never told me that."

Granddaddy nodded his head. "Yup. I wrestled for a couple of years before I enlisted. I wasn't as good as you are, but I had a couple of moves that worked pretty well. Years later, I got to spend some time with former United States Olympic wrestling coach Jim Peckham. He was coaching a group of high school wrestlers on a few moves, and one of the kids asked if he could show him a variation he'd come up with.

"Coach Peckham said yes, even though he could have just as easily said no. He didn't know who the kid was, and truth be told, it was probably a little cocky of the kid to think he was going to show Jim Peckham something he didn't already know.

"I don't remember what I thought would happen, but I remember what did happen. He watched the kid, and when he was done, Coach Peckham smiled and said that his way was a good way to do the move. Then he laughed and said, 'The day you stop learning, is the day you should hang it up.' Like other things I heard when I was younger, it took a while to sink in, but I get it now. Live to learn and you'll learn to live."

Granddaddy turned and looked at me. "That's why I know you'll be a great coach. You've already shown how much you love to learn. At some point you're going to want to share what you've learned with other people. As soon as you start coaching, you're going to realize it's a two-way street. They get something out of it, but you do too. When you're coaching, you're helping people reach for their dreams. Now, I don't know who you're going to coach. It might be kids; it might be your peers. Either way, I know you'll be great at it."

"You don't think it's too late for me to learn how to be a good coach?"

"Not at all, Dakota. You're only 16. What would stop you from being a good coach?"

I looked down at the ground again and shrugged. "I don't know... I've read stuff that says my brain is already set in its ways, so it would be harder for me to learn stuff because I'm so old... and... maybe I'm not smart enough."

Granddaddy put his hand on my shoulder. "Let's be very clear about something here. Learning doesn't require a high I.Q. It requires interest, intention, and attention. If you aren't interested in something, it's not going to matter how smart you are. But when you have an *intention* of pursuing your dreams and you start paying *attention* to what there is to learn about it, your brain will cooperate and start absorbing the information you're feeding it.

"Your brain craves information. Think about a video game you really liked. I bet you learned how to play that easily enough. Don't ever believe you aren't smart enough to learn. Insight, common sense, wisdom, and experience are just as important as lessons in a book, and that's something you'll figure out when you start reading. And plenty of those books will be written about, or by, people who weren't superstars at everything they did in school. You know who

Albert Einstein is, right?" I nodded.

"It's interesting because a lot of people believe he got bad grades in school but still became a Nobel Prize winner. He did win the prize, but he didn't do bad in school. His math and science scores were very high. What happened was that he was so into science that all his non-science grades suffered. He did so badly in his French classes that it delayed his entry into the school he wanted to go to by one year." "Really?" I asked.

"Really. Richard Branson, the guy who built Virgin Records, Virgin Atlantic Airways, and Virgin Mobile, dropped out of high school when he was 16, but look at what he's accomplished. Abraham Lincoln was a lawyer and a president with only one year of formal schooling. The world is full of people who succeeded without the advantages of a formal education."

Granddaddy stopped and turned to look at me. "But let's be clear, I'm not saying that dropping out of school is a good choice. The point I'm trying to make is that most people are smart enough when they're interested enough. You're no different. Chances are you might become an expert in wrestling first, but that's proof you have the ability to learn.

"If you want to be one of those people who reaches for more in life, that's even easier to do. Don't fool yourself into thinking there isn't anything else worth learning. Learn from others. Expand the knowledge they've shared with you by adding it to what you've learned from your life's experiences, and then make sure to share what you've learned with others so they have something they can expand on with their experiences."

"Kind of like a relay race, only instead of passing a baton between us, we're passing knowledge."

"Again, you nailed it. Seriously, being able to make that kind of observation of how one thing is similar to another, that's a very impressive thing to be able to do. I couldn't do that when I was your age. I can now, though. Like I said, success isn't just about smarts. It's about desire and commitment too."

"I get what you're saying and I'm psyched to start reading more about some of the people you talked about today."

"Who would you start with?"

"I'm not sure. Maybe Napoleon," I said and then continued. "I remember you saying that Napoleon and I had things in common. We both won a lot of fights to prove we could do more than people said we could. We didn't crack under the pressure we felt, either. Instead, we both turned that negativity into a drive and a commitment to succeed."

"True," said Granddaddy.

He sounded impressed so I kept talking. "I like that. He's my new boy now! I already feel like we have a lot in common."

"Is he the only person?" Granddaddy asked.

"No," I hesitated, but then confessed, "but I have a tough time remembering names sometimes. There was one other guy you were telling me about. The one who lived around the same time as Jesus?"

"Cicero?" Granddaddy asked.

"Yeah. That's his name. Cicero. I'll try and remember it. Cicero."

Granddaddy gave me a questioning look. "What's the deal with names?"

"Sometimes I have a hard time remembering them. Like... I remember wrestlers when I see them, but it's easier for me to remember their moves than it is to remember their names." I paused, but didn't wait for Granddaddy to say what he was probably thinking. "I know that's not good. But I get a lot of people coming up to me at work, or wherever, and they start talking to me about sports. It's hard for me to remember all their names."

"So maybe names will be one of those things you have to work a little harder on because names are very important. Learning someone's name is a sign of respect. It lets people know they aren't invisible to you. I know you might not know what that feels like because so many people know you by name, but for the people talking to you, it won't always be the same. Think about what it might mean to a first year wrestler to have you remember his name once you become an Olympic wrestler. How will that kid feel about himself when you re-member his name?"

The thought of it made me smile. It got me thinking about signing autographs too. Did I really need to know everybody's name for that? Maybe not for autographs, but Granddaddy was wrong when he said I didn't know what it was like to feel in-visible. I knew exactly what it felt like to have people looking at you or through you like you didn't exist. I didn't like the thought of making someone else feel like that just because I couldn't remember his or her name.

Granddaddy interrupted my thoughts. "You can find lots of tricks for remembering people's names online. And here's another reason to remember people's names. Hammurabi, Ramses the Great, Charles Darwin, Alexander the Great, Julius Caesar, Elizabeth I, Confucius, Sir Isaac Newton, Christopher Columbus, Benjamin Franklin, Andrew Jackson, Crazy Horse, Anne Frank, Tecumseh, Abraham Lincoln, Harriet Tubman, Albert Einstein, Rosa Parks,

Sigmund Freud, Gandhi, Malcolm X, and Susan B. Anthony." I just looked at him. "Do I have to remember all those names?"

"When you start reading about people it will be easier than it seems right now. Look, we both know you won't actually be meeting any of the people I just named because... well... because they're all dead; so it might not seem like their names are important. But each of them was a living, breathing person at one time too, and if their experience and knowledge helps us make more sense or success out of our lives, the least we can do is respect them by remembering their names. As far as remembering the names of people who are alive, that's just plain respectful. There are a lot of secrets I'm sharing with you today that might take a while to sink in, but I hope this isn't one of them. This is one you can do something about right now."

"I know Jenn will appreciate it."

"How do you know that?"

"She gets so mad at me because sometimes we'll be out somewhere and someone will start talking to me and I don't introduce her." I held my hand up to Granddaddy. "I know what you're going to say and you're right, but the reason I don't introduce them is because I can't remember their name. I don't know how to ask, and I don't want them to know I forgot. Of course my girl... Jenn gets mad because she thinks I'm not introducing her to them. I've tried to explain it, and I think she understands, but that doesn't stop her from feeling left out."

"Invisible?"

"Oh man, I hope not. You're right. I've got to get on top of this. You said there's stuff online I can learn from?"

"There's always stuff online you can learn from, and learning ways to remember people's names is a good place for something like that. But don't get hooked on doing all your learning online. Books are good too. There's something nice about having a book in your hand. They're real. It's easier to read pages and sections more than once, and easier to go back to different sections of the book when you want to check something. You can take them with you too."

"Yeah, but books are expensive. I lost a school book last year and had to pay $25!"

"Don't you have a library card?"

"Yeah, I do, but the library?" I moaned.

"Yes, the library. I know it may not seem like the hippest place to hang out, but no one says you have to hang out there. All I'm suggesting is that all the people I mentioned, and all the people you're going to decide you want to learn more about, are in books you'll find in the library. And think about it, if you start there, it won't cost you a dime to spend time with those amazing people, their thoughts, their accomplishments, or their ideas.

"If you don't want to spend time in the library, you can probably go to the library's website first, pick the book you want to read, and have them hold it for you at the front desk. That way you can run in, check the book out, run out, and in less than a couple of minutes you'll be able to start reading about one of your new friends."

"Okay. I really do want to do this stuff. I'll do it," I said, smiling at Granddaddy, suddenly remembering something I was curious about.

"What do you want to know?" he asked.

"I know you quit school to join the Army, and I know you went back to school, but I don't know what you did exactly. Did you graduate?"

Granddaddy looked thoughtful for a bit. "I did graduate... from high school and college. And I'm going to tell you something I don't always share with other people because some people think

I'm bragging when I say it, but I have a few degrees."

"Really? What are they?"

"I have doctorates in both history and political science."

"Wow. I figured you were really smart."

Granddaddy shook his head. "That's one of the reasons I don't always tell people. They hear about my degrees and then they automatically think I'm smarter than them and that my education puts me above them. It doesn't. All it means is that I wanted to learn more. I wanted the challenge of learning and that's what school does sometimes. It challenges us to push the limits of what we know and understand."

I knew I had that confused look on my face again, but I couldn't help it.

"You actually understand this and I'll prove it to you. Remember how we talked about learning all the names and dates and stuff so you can pass a test?" I nodded.

"Well the difference I'm talking about is when you know the names and dates, but you also understand how the story fits in there too. So when I got my degrees, I wasn't just learning more names and dates. I was learning how everything fit together. For example, obviously, I love history. But once I started learning by looking at all the information that was available, it was even more amazing. It was like I was there when they were devising strategies and making plans.

"The subjects you choose to dive into might be different for you. You might really like studying athletes. They're amazing to read about too, and when you're able to connect the story with the person, their accomplishments become real and tangible things. The point is, the only thing my degrees are evidence of is the fact that I was committed and inspired to learn more about how the world got to where it is today. History didn't make me smarter than anyone else. But when I gave myself permission to learn from it, it taught me how to live today."

GIVE YOURSELF PERMISSION!

"I am determined to be cheerful and happy in whatever situation I may find myself. For I have learned that the greater part of our misery or unhappiness is determined not by our circumstance, but by our disposition."
—Martha Washington 1731-1802,
First Lady of the United States

I wondered if I'd heard him right. "So you gave yourself permission to learn?"

"Sure did, Dakota," Granddaddy replied.

"I don't get it. How can you give yourself permission to do something? Don't you just do it, or don't do it?"

"People either do something or don't do something, that's true, but giving yourself *permission* to do something or to not do something can change your whole experience."

"That doesn't make sense," I said shaking my head.

"Sure it does. Have you ever gone to a movie you weren't the least bit interested in seeing?" Granddaddy asked.

I rolled my eyes. "Chick flicks. Jenn loves them, but she doesn't want to go see them with her girlfriends. She always wants me to go with her."

"I hear you. I've been to my share of chick flicks too," Granddaddy said, shaking his head. "But let me ask you this.

What do you think would happen if you gave yourself permission to find something about the whole experience you could enjoy? Like giving yourself permission to enjoy spending this time with Jenn without having to think up things to talk about? Or giving yourself permission to see how happy it makes her when you take her to a movie she really wants to see."

"I've never thought of doing it like that."

"Give it a try. I can pretty much guarantee it will change your experience when you do," Granddaddy said. "Very few things in life are 100 percent fun, even when you're really passionate about the goals they lead to. A while back you said you really liked working out, but there must be something you don't like to do. What is it?"

"Squats... Ugh."

"The next time you're working out and you have to do squats, try giving yourself permission to not love doing it, but also make sure to remind yourself that by choosing to do it anyway, even one of your least favorite things to do is helping you achieve your dreams."

Granddaddy turned to face me. "Sitting around and waiting for the world to give you permission to be more than you are is a waste of time. Think about it. If everyone is waiting for someone else to take charge and give them permission to be motivated, then who's left to take charge?"

"No one." I understood.

"That's right. No one. But that's what happens most of the time. People look everywhere else for permission to believe in their dreams, and when they don't get it, they give up. Even if they do get started, the next worst thing usually happens. They accomplish something and then they look at the people around them hoping for approval and recognition. If they don't get it, they give up because this time they're waiting for someone else to give them permission to enjoy their accomplishment. Either way, they're right back where they started."

"I think I understand what you're saying. There's a guy on my wrestling team... he's ranked second right behind me. But he's never happy when he wins. I think it's because his dad is always giving him a hard time. He gives him dirty looks when he loses and barely smiles when he wins. I've congratulated him before, but all he does is shrug his shoulders. He doesn't smile, either. Do you think it's because he hasn't given himself permission to enjoy his wins?"

"It sounds like it. There's probably other stuff going on there too. But I'd be willing to bet that if it had started differently, if he had felt like his dad was happy with his progress from the beginning, he'd probably have been able to give himself permission to enjoy his wins too."

"That's a pretty cool way to look at it. I'm going to try that the next time I take Jenn to the movies. If I can figure out a movie she wants to see, I might even ask her if she wants to go before she brings it up. I bet that would make her really happy."

Granddaddy looked at me. "You're smiling."

"Sure. I feel good. Why shouldn't I smile?"

"Just wanted to bring it to your attention. A minute ago you were rolling your eyes thinking about chick flicks, but as soon as you gave yourself permission to find some aspect of it you could feel good about, you came up with a win-win scenario for both you and Jenn."

"Huh. So whenever I have to do something I don't want to do—" "Or can't do something you want to do—" Granddaddy added. "I just have to give myself permission to find something about the situation I can feel good about?"

"Yup," Granddaddy said. "And as you begin to notice how many people around you don't know how to do this, my prediction is that you're going to start giving the people around you permission too."

"But I thought you were saying that other people can't give us permission."

"You're right, they can't. But when someone acknowledges our efforts, it can be enough to get us moving in the right direction. One of the reasons people don't do this is because no one ever told them it was an option. That's why I think you'll be a great coach. You'll see people succeed, but when you tell them what a good job they're doing, you'll make sure they realize that their accomplishments were the result of the work they put in. They aren't the result of a coach saying it, or because they earned a check mark in the 'win' column. You'll be encouraging them and giving them permission to acknowledge the effects their efforts have had on their success." "I think I can do that."

"I think you can too. And that's one of the skills that will make you a good leader."

"You think I'll be a good leader?"

"It's part of your plan."

"Yeah, but... you know... I hadn't really thought it through yet... like how I would do it."

Granddaddy raised his eyebrows. "You may not have planned out all the A-B-Cs of what kind of leader you want to be, but believe me, you already possess a lot of the skills. And don't get stuck on the idea that all leaders have titles. There are plenty of great leaders in this world whose only titles are mom or dad. Good leaders inspire the people around them to believe in themselves and their abilities. They give credit where credit is due, encourage when times are tough, and are happy to celebrate victories regardless of how big or small they are."

I smiled. "Then you must be a good leader because talking to you makes me feel like I can do just about anything."

"Why would you think you couldn't?" Granddaddy asked.

"I guess because it seems like there aren't many people who ever get what they really want." I looked at Granddaddy. "I think you did, but I don't think pops did. I don't know if mom did, but it's hard to believe she wanted what she's got. I don't know what my brother wanted either, but I don't think it was jail."

"It sounds a little bit like you still have doubts about your plan."

"It's more like I know where I want to go, but I also know that people shoot for things all the time and miss. I work harder because I don't want to miss." I looked down at the ground. "But what if I fail?"

"That's a good question, and I'm glad you had the courage to ask it out loud." Granddaddy paused for a minute before continuing. "Things do happen, and they aren't always good. But what you're really talking about is fear of the unknown, and that's something I know a lot about. When we were fighting Hitler, we always had a plan before we made a move, but there were never any guarantees we would be successful. All we could do was commit to bringing our best to the action. It was interesting thinking about it that way too, because it got us very focused, similar to the way you get focused with your sports."

"Uh... I think your situation was a little more important than mine."

"From a historical perspective maybe, but from an individual perspective, it really isn't much different. We make plans we believe will help us accomplish our goal, but the possibility of failure is always there. The question is, which would you rather do—bring your best to the plan and face it head-on regardless of the outcome?

Or plan to bring your best but then let your fears and doubts interfere with your ability to bring your best?"

"I'd rather bring my best."

"That's what Colonel Reynolds taught me to do. When he talked to us about what was going to happen next, he never wasted one breath trying to convince us everything would be okay. Instead, he reminded us of how capable and accomplished we were. He reminded us that we were strong and capable as individuals, as a group, and in our belief in what we were fighting for. That's what we took into battle with us.

"I know that may sound more important than stepping out onto a wrestling mat, but don't kid yourself. Every time we step up to a challenge, failure is always an option regardless of how big or small or unimportant the challenge may seem. Do you know who Vince Lombardi was?"

"Sure. Coach of the Green Bay Packers."

"Right. Well he said it doesn't matter how many times you get knocked down, what matters is how many times you get back up. He understood that the difference between winning and losing wasn't always about actually winning the contest.

Take wrestling, for example. You expend a lot of energy and effort when you're out there wrestling, but think back to when you first started. Think about those early practices and matches and remember what it felt like. Did you feel like you were fighting for your life out there? Do you remember feeling like you'd gotten hit by a Mack truck after a match regardless of whether you'd lost or won?"

"It makes my body ache thinking about it," I said, wincing.

"Do you remember what it felt like when you started getting tired during a match and how it felt like your lungs were on fire and about to burst while you're trying to keep up with your opponent? You had to keep going, but the more tired you got, the harder it was to feel like you could see it through. And then a thought zaps into your head—what if I can't do this? Do I have what it takes to win?" Granddaddy shook his head. "I don't know about you, but I remember it."

"I know what you're talking about. It happened to me a couple of times in the beginning. I panicked because I realized it wasn't going well, and I started thinking about losing. I didn't want to lose, but then it was like I was frozen and I had a hard time getting my body to cooperate."

"What happened?" Granddaddy asked.

"I lost."

"And then how did you feel?"

"Well, I felt like crawling off into a corner. I don't know...

I guess I felt like I'd failed. I really wanted to win. But I didn't."

"So why didn't you quit?"

GOT EXCUSES?

---

*"People who are unable to motivate themselves
must be content with mediocrity, no matter how
impressive their other talents."*
—Andrew Carnegie

I stared at him. "Why would I quit?"

"Because you didn't win."

"Yeah, but I'd been working really hard. I wasn't going to quit because I didn't win one match. I just kept trying to get better... and I did."

Granddaddy nodded his head. "And I think that's what Lombardi was talking about. That's what we do when we get really tired and feel like we've reached our limit. Sometimes it's easier to give up than it is to keep going and lose. Sometimes it's easier to stay down than it is to risk losing the dream."

I frowned and nodded. "I know what you're talking about."

"How so?" Granddaddy asked.

"I've been there. But after losing a few times I decided I was going to do what I had to do to win."

"And what did you decide you had to do?"

"Obviously I had to work harder to get stronger. I started paying more attention to what other wrestlers were doing, looking for things I could take advantage of. Stuff like that. But mostly I decided to win. As soon as I made that decision, I started to win." Granddaddy chuckled.

"Why are you laughing?" I asked feeling offended.

Granddaddy shrugged. "Because I'm always amazed when people say they just decided to *win*, or to *be the best*, or *number one*, and then when they finally get there, they think it's because they made a decision to do it."

"What's wrong with deciding to be the best?"

"Nothing... nothing at all. Making the decision to be the best is an admirable quest. It's just a tough goal because you don't really have any control when it comes down to winning or losing."

"What do you mean? I'm the number-one wrestler on my team and I got there because I decided I wanted it."

"No. You got to number one because you did the work that put you in a position to challenge for the number-one spot. The fact that you won doesn't have anything to do with your ability to choose to win."

I shook my head. "You aren't making any sense. I decided I had to win, I did what I had to do to win, and I won."

"Okay, but what would have happened if you'd done all your preparation, done your very best on the mat, and still lost? What would have happened then?"

"But that's not what happened. I won."

"I get that, Dakota. But what would have happened if you'd lost?"

I didn't understand what Granddaddy wanted me to say. Did he want me to say I wasn't as good as I thought I was? Well that wasn't going to happen because I knew I was good—

very good. And as long as I kept working hard, I knew I was going to keep getting better. I tossed my hands in the air.

"I don't know what you want me to say."

Granddaddy shrugged. "All I'm saying is that it's easy to put your talent and skill to the test when you're winning, but don't let winning become the prize you use as motivation to keep going.

The fact is, you don't have any control over who's going to win."

"Sure I do. That's how I win, by taking control on the mat."

"Okay. So let's agree to disagree right now. And don't change what you've been doing, because it's working. Absolutely keep deciding to win. Just think about what I said and understand that there are a lot of ways to win a contest that can't be measured by the weight of the trophy you hold up at the end." It was my turn to laugh.

"Why are you laughing?" Granddaddy laughed.

I shook my head. "Because sometimes the things you say sound like something you'd find in a fortune cookie."

Granddaddy nodded and laughed too. "You're right. Sometimes they do... But that doesn't mean they aren't important."

"Is that why you're harping on my decision to win?"

"Not at all. But once again, I have to remind you that you're an exception. Most people don't win. They start out the same way you did, by making an effort and putting their talent, skill, and goals to the test... and not just with sports. But if they don't win, they start being afraid to put themselves out there and really try to reach for something meaningful. Their losses hit them hard and then they give up. They don't dare risk their dreams by trying to achieve them because if they fail, and lose their dream in the process, they'll feel like they've lost every-thing."

"That's so sad. All they have to do is keep working. But I've seen it on the wrestling team too. Guys try out and they have some talent and do the work, but then they lose a couple of times and quit. I've never understood that. It's like they quit without ever really trying."

"Maybe it's because they've been led to believe winning is the most important part of the contest—the only thing that mat-ters. People who believe that usually decide it's safer not to try to win than it is to risk it all and lose."

"I thought about that too in the beginning. After losing those first few matches, I felt whipped in every way. I could barely move. My head felt like it weighed 100 pounds and my muscles felt like rubber. Come to think of it, I still feel like that sometimes, but I don't think about it the same way anymore. I just accept it as part of the process."

"Maybe so, but you did something not everyone knows how to do. Instead of giving in to the pain and discomfort wres-tling forces you to endure by quitting, you made the choice to deal with it and still continued to do more."

"You have to do more if you want to succeed. The more I do, the better my overall results are. It's kind of a no-brainer."

Granddaddy smiled. "I agree. But people don't learn to think like that. When they don't get the results they want, they start thinking it's because the other guy had something they don't. A lot of coaches say things like 'That's okay. We'll get them next time' or 'Good effort,' but those kinds of words don't help.

"The fact is, losses are tough subjects and people don't know how to talk about them. It's easier to chalk it up to things like shifts in momentum, a lucky break, the crowd was on the other team's side, or they had the 'home team' advantage. Those things sound good, but you can't compete against those kinds of excuses. You can't succeed if you start looking at your results and decide they were caused by things you have no control over. And this doesn't just apply to sports."

"What do you mean?" I asked.

"How about this situation? How many times have you heard kids in school complain about getting a bad grade on a test?"

"All the time," I answered.

"Kids will complain about a bad grade and come up with all kinds of excuses to explain it. The teacher was unfair, there were questions on the test we hadn't covered in class, or the questions were trick questions."

"You missed a few," I said, laughing. "The teacher didn't review the material. They weren't given enough time to study, or because of sports or work, or the test was too hard."

"So it sounds like it's pretty easy to avoid the real reason for a bad grade if all those other excuses are available."

"I guess so." I shrugged. "I know what you're getting at here. You're trying to get me to see that if I want to get better grades I have to work harder instead of coming up with excuses like the ones we just came up with."

"I wasn't talking about you. I brought it up as an example of how easy it is to look at results and blame other people and situations for them. That's what people have learned to do.

Your teachers will remind you that studying will result in better grades, but they always say that."

"It's like a broken record," I said rolling my eyes.

"So why don't kids take their teachers' advice and study harder?"

"Because teachers care about grades. Some teachers are nicer than others, and it's easier to learn in some classes, but I'm not sure they really care about what we learn. I know they care about how good our grades are. If we do really bad, they look bad, so they get on our cases about studying."

"So that means if you get a bad grade it's their fault because..."

"Because they shouldn't harass us about studying. Maybe they shouldn't always blame us if we get a bad grade. Maybe if they treated us differently..."

Granddaddy continued my thought for me. "You'd get better grades?"

I shrugged. "Maybe."

"But if you could get better grades without them asking you to study, or if they treated you differently, doesn't that mean you could get better grades anyway?"

I didn't want to answer because once again Granddaddy was right.

"That's okay, you don't have to answer. I can tell by your expression that you get it. You know your grades aren't the result of a teacher trying to get you to study. The decision to study always was, always is, always will be a choice you get to make. The challenge is looking at the situation and deciding where you want to put your energy. Do you want to invest it in studying, or do you want to invest it in rebelling against a teacher?

"You can even take it one step further and think about the results you'll get with both situations. Which result would you feel better about? A better grade that's the result of your effort, or a bad grade that gives you the opportunity to put the blame on someone else?"

I looked at Granddaddy. "Don't you think you're pushing it a little bit here? I don't think like that."

Granddaddy shrugged. "Maybe not. But I wanted to give you a really good example of a situation where people give up their own power to succeed simply because they've learned it's easier to blame other people for their failure than it is to step up and take control of their own results."

"Do you think everybody can get good grades?"

"I don't know if everybody can get better grades. I know there's a difference between setting a goal and making an effort to accomplish it, and being either too scared or too lazy to try. And those are the two extremes people get stuck between. Teachers, coaches, and mentors can give their students advice, just like bosses can tell their employees how to do something. But it always comes down to the choices we make when we're deciding how to respond."

Granddaddy sighed. "People waste so much time blaming the world for their situations. They wish things were different, but the answer is always right there in front of them."

I suddenly wondered if Granddaddy was about to expose one great big secret that would be the answer to everything we were talking about today.

"What answer?" I asked, totally hoping to be blown away.

"GOYA."

GOYA

*"It doesn't matter how many times you fail.
It doesn't matter how many times you almost get it right.
No one is going to know or care about your failures, and neither should you. All you have to do is learn from them and
those around you. All that matters in business is that you get
it right once."*
—Mark Cuban, entrepreneur, author, and owner of
the NBA's Dallas Mavericks

"What?"

"GOYA," Granddaddy repeated. "Get off your ass." I
turned away from him and started laughing.

"You think that's funny?" He asked.

"You said ass," I said, laughing.

Granddaddy started laughing too. "You're right. I did. But
I said a little bit more than that. Have you ever heard of GOYA
before?" I shook my head no.

Granddaddy was still smiling, but he looked out into the
rain. "I'm not surprised," he said, sounding discouraged.
"Ideas like GOYA could make such a difference if people
heard about them... if they understood them."

Even though it didn't sound like the one big secret I was
hoping for, Granddaddy hadn't let me down yet today.

"So how does GOYA work?"

Granddaddy raised his eyebrows. "I would have thought you knew exactly how it worked."

"Well... sure. I know what it means. It means getting off your ass." I tried to sound serious, but I started laughing again.

Granddaddy smiled, but he didn't laugh this time.

Instead, he turned, looked at me and asked, "But how do you get started? In one way it seems like getting up and doing something would be the easiest thing in the world to do. But it can be a real challenge coming up with a meaningful reason to GOYA and do something."

"I think I have a meaningful reason," I said. At least I wanted to believe I did.

"What is it?"

I opened my mouth, but then stopped. My original reason was to stop Pops, but it turned out I hadn't needed to protect myself. So why was I still doing what I was doing? All of a sudden I wasn't so sure. I kept going because sports gave me something to do that I was good at and was getting better at. But I didn't know if that was a meaningful reason for doing something. I looked at Granddaddy and shrugged.

"I thought I had meaningful reasons," I said. "But now I don't know if they're *meaningful*. They're definitely reasons why I do things, but are they *meaningful*? That word makes me think that maybe my reasons aren't deep enough. Like... is getting a trophy meaningful?" I looked at Granddaddy and then looked away. "Now I'm thinking my reasons might not be good reasons."

Granddaddy smiled and clapped a hand on my shoulder. "And now you know how easy it is for people to end up feeling like their dreams and goals aren't worth pursuing. All it took was one question from me to get you to question whether or not your reasons are meaningful."

That shook me right down to the soles of my feet. I didn't think anybody could get me to second guess myself, but he was right. He'd done it with one question.

"But how do I know if my reasons are good enough reasons... like you said... if they're meaningful?"

Granddaddy looked thoughtful. "That's a very good question, but it's a tough one too because it isn't up to me to decide. Only you can decide if your reasons are meaningful. That's one of the reasons people struggle with applying GOYA to their lives. They look to their family and friends and hope to hear things like, 'Yes. Your reasons are meaningful. Go for it!' But that's not what they hear. Look at your situation. How many people have you told your reasons to?"

I shook my head. "I've never talked about it with anyone before today." I stared down at the floor. "Not even Jenn," I whispered.

"I totally understand. When I was your age I didn't have as much drive as you have, but I didn't tell anyone what I was doing, either. I joined the Army for one reason— to get away from my dad. After I'd enlisted, I had a new reason to take action—to protect our country. But when that was done, I struggled with what to do next. There were plenty of people telling me what I should do, but nothing felt right—or good— on the inside."

"What'd you do?"

"I did what most people do when that happens... I sat around with a bunch of guys in the same situation and complained right along with them."

"Really?" I was having a hard time imagining Granddaddy being like that.

"Sure. It was easy to sit and complain about how hard things were, how much I hated my job, how tight money was, how tired I was, and how no one really appreciated me. They all nodded their heads and agreed with me, and I did the same when they complained about their lives. But then one day I was listening to this older guy complaining, just like we always did, and I got mad. Not at him, exactly; I was just tired of hearing him say the same things day after day and almost told him that if he didn't like the way things were then he should get off his ass and do something about it."

Granddaddy looked thoughtful. "I distinctly remember opening my mouth and closing it and looking at him, and it was like I was staring at myself, only I was 30 years older." Granddaddy looked down at the ground. "It scared the crap out of me." "Wow. That's crazy," I said.

"Tell me about it, Dakota. But suddenly I had a reason. I didn't want to end up like that guy. I knew I wanted more, and right then and there, I realized that if I wanted a better life, it was up to me. It was sad too, because I also realized that if I kept hanging around with those guys, they'd be able to drag me right back to where they were.

"I liked them. They were good guys, and deciding to stop hanging out with them was definitely one of the hardest parts. I still thought of them as my friends, but I understood that we were going in different directions now. I could have tried to get them to join me, but people aren't like that. I'd found a new reason to make an effort, but they'd given up looking for a better reason to take action a long time ago."

"Wow." That was all I could say. It was so strange to hear that Granddaddy hadn't started out like he was now. He'd struggled when he was young too, and I wondered what he was like back then. Was he like his dad? Or had he been like Pops was now?

"Hey," Granddaddy said interrupting my thoughts. "I didn't tell you that so you'd feel sorry for me. I told you because it's important to understand that the reasons people do what they do are personal. There isn't one good or perfect reason. There's only the reason that motivates *you* to move in a better direction."

"So what'd you do?"

Granddaddy rubbed his chin. "That's a long story for another day. Right now it's almost time for you to go to work, and there are a couple more things we have to cover before we're done."

"Okay," I said, but I was disappointed because I really wanted to hear more about what Granddaddy had done in his life.

"There's one more thing I want you to know about the time I spent with those guys back then, and it's going to sound strange, but we were happy." Granddaddy shook his head and chuckled. "Sometimes it's easy to look at a group of people and think that they have to be unhappy because of where they are and how they're living, but that's a mistake. People can be rich and unhappy, or poor and happy. I didn't have any money back then, didn't really have any ambition, but we had a good time all the same.

"I think the difference between me and the guys I was hanging out with was simply that I hadn't given up yet. I'd had some experience with success and it had made an impression on me. I wanted to be successful. I liked the feeling of it. I wasn't exactly sure what I wanted to succeed at yet, but I really believed it would make me happy, so I'd found my reason to start pursuing happiness elsewhere."

Granddaddy turned to me. "Dakota, people get to decide what makes them happy. You get to decide what makes you happy. The same goes with what you choose to do. You get to decide what feels right, or meaningful, or purposeful. No one else can give you those things. No one else can tell you *what* to do to feel them, either—because it's not *what* you do that matters. Let me rephrase that last part. What you do in life can matter a great deal to other people, but what's going to matter to you is how you feel when you do it. When you feel like the things you're doing are making a contribution to some aspect of life, then even the smallest contribution can be meaningful."

I was trying to follow what he was saying, but I was getting a little lost. "It doesn't matter what I do? How can that be?"

"If *what* we did was the source of our happiness, then it wouldn't matter what we did. We'd all be happy regardless of what we were doing. People make that mistake a lot. They think that doing bigger things, like owning their own company, will make them happier.

It just isn't true."

"But I want to own my own company someday too. What's wrong with that?" I asked a little defensively.

"Nothing," Granddaddy replied. "It's a good goal, but owning your own company is no guarantee of happiness. Happiness isn't the result of *what* you do. It's the result of *how* you do it."

"Huh?"

"What you do will never be as meaningful, or memorable, or as motivating as how you do it. Look at it like this. Over the past couple of years you've started collecting trophies. When you look at them, what do you think about?"

I shrugged. "I don't know... maybe that it was cool that I won."

"Fair enough. Now think about all those athletes you've heard about who took illegal steroids. Do you think they feel the same thing as you do when they look at their trophies?"

"I doubt it. They cheated. They may have the trophy, but they didn't win it fair and square. If I were them, I wouldn't be able to look at them."

"So you think something different when you look at your trophies."

"I guess so. At least I didn't cheat. I worked really hard to get them."

"How do you feel about all the extra work you did in the gym? I know it was hard, I know you hate squats, and I know you don't get a trophy every time you compete regardless of how many extra squats you did. So why do you keep doing it?"

"I don't know. It may sound weird, but I like the work. I like the physical part of it and I like the challenge when I step on the mat. I know I don't win every time, but when I do win, I like the trophy too."

"It sounds like wrestling is hard work. I know why you started doing it, but now that you know you can take care of yourself, why do you keep doing it?"

I hesitated but then answered. "This is going to sound even weirder, but I'm kind of addicted to it. If I go too many days without working out, I feel like a slug. Jenn says I get grouchy when I don't work out. As soon as I work out, I feel great again."

"Well, maybe that's what happens when people get used to doing what they're doing. It's such a habit, that it becomes more like an addiction. I think that's what happened to the guys I hung out with after the Army. They were so used to complaining day after day that they couldn't go a day without complaining. They kept complaining because they couldn't come up with a good enough reason not to."

"They weren't motivated," I said.

"What do you mean?" Granddaddy asked.

"Um... If I wasn't getting the results I wanted, I'd try and figure out what else I could do to improve my results. That's how I started winning wrestling matches. I figured out what I needed to do to improve. I'd work on it to get better. It worked too. I started winning more. If your old buddies weren't interested in doing more, then either they were happy right where they were, or they weren't motivated enough to try something new." I frowned. "So instead of doing something new, they just kept doing what they always did."

"Exactly!" Granddaddy exclaimed. "Einstein nailed this situation right on the head when he said, 'We cannot solve our problems with the same thinking we used when we created them.' These days people call that the definition of insanity."

"Doing the same thing over and over again and expecting a different result," I interrupted.

"Yup. Thinking outside the box is another phrase people use too, but they all boil down to the same thing. If you want something beyond what you have right now, then you have to open your mind to new ideas—like reading. If you don't, you'll spend your life rearranging what you already know. As soon as you start looking outside of yourself, you'll begin to see how many things are possible. You might even discover a path you'll love every step of."

"You're talking about comfort zones. I know what those are.

Comfort zones are for losers."

WHEN YOU HELP OTHERS, YOU HELP YOURSELF!

"There is no exercise better for the heart than reaching down and lifting people up." —John Holmes

"That sounds a little harsh, Dakota," Granddaddy said.

I shook my head. "I disagree. One of my coaches talked to the team about losing one day. We'd lost a few matches in a row and he wasn't happy. We thought he was going to yell at us, but he didn't. Instead, he talked about how comfortable couches can be, and how when we sit there watching TV or playing video games, the distance between us and our dreams keeps growing. After a while, our dreams start to feel like they're a million miles away and it's easier to put them out of our mind than it is to figure out how to get started.

"Then he asked us to think about people we know who spent most of their free time sitting on the couch doing nothing but watching TV or playing video games. He told us to imagine what they might look like in 20 years. Or what we might look like in 20 years if we decided to sit down and join them. It was a pretty scary thought. All I could see was Pops drinking a beer and yelling at some sports team on TV."

Granddaddy nodded his head. "It's a good analogy, but I bet there were still people who didn't respond." "A couple," I said.

"Some people are too scared to make a move. It's probably the saddest thing to have happen too, but it happens all the same. Momentum helps, and that's one thing winning does accomplish. It helps build momentum. You do some work, you get some good results, your confidence builds, you keep working, you win more, et cetera. It's easier to keep momentum going with sports, though."

Granddaddy smiled at me. "There are a lot more trophies in sports than there are in life. That's why reasons are so important. If you don't have good reasons for pursuing your goals, it's very hard to stay motivated long enough to see them through."

"I get that, but why don't people do something? Why don't they just get off their... ah... butts and do something?"

"If it was that simple, they probably would. But they'd have to believe there was something better out there, and a lot of people have let that ship sail. Or they've decided they're too old, or too dumb, or that it will take too much work, or that there's no one to step in and help them, or whatever. Some people don't think they deserve anything better. But sometimes it's simply because they're too afraid to step outside their comfort zone—even when their comfort zone is in a bad place.

"It's like trying to believe the world is round when everyone around you is still convinced it's flat. You believe the world is round, you believe the people around you are wrong, but look at the risk you're taking if you start walking. You're walking away from everything and everyone you know towards something completely unknown and foreign to you. And most of the time you're walking alone. It takes a lot of faith and inner strength to start walking down that path."

"I hadn't thought about it like that before. So... how do you convince unmotivated or scared people to do something?" I asked.

"*You* can't. People have to make that decision on their own. And it's not like they can't survive if they don't make the decision to reach for something better. In this country we take care of people who are struggling. It's sad, but there are people who take advantage of those services, blaming everybody else for their problems. After a while, that becomes their comfort zone."

"But that's wrong. You can't go around blaming other people for your situation."

Granddaddy shrugged. "It's risky business to blame people for the situation they're in too. You might be right, but you don't know their situations or their circumstances. It's just as easy to blame people from a distance for their problems as it is for them to blame you from a distance for not doing anything to help them. It sets up a lose-lose situation where nothing ever changes."

"I don't get it. Then what's the answer?"

"The best answer is always to take action. G-O-Y-A and do something—anything!"

"But people don't," I said. "I see that. Heck, sometimes I don't do anything."

"Me too. Sometimes I don't do anything, either." I stared at him in disbelief.

"You get stuck too?"

"Sure," Granddaddy replied. "I'm human. Back when I was really stuck I came up with a good reason to take action. But it's impossible to stay motivated all the time. There are times when you need a break. The real trick is not letting that break last too long. The longer it lasts, the harder it is to get back into the groove. Take your workouts for example. If you didn't work out for a month, what would happen?"

I thought about it. "It would hurt. I'd have lost a lot of ground in a month and wouldn't be very competitive at that point. I'd probably lose matches until I was back in shape." I looked at Granddaddy. "It would suck."

Granddaddy nodded his head. "It sure would. That's why it's important to have things you can do that keep you moving even if you aren't motivated to work on your own stuff at the moment. And, there's one sure-fire action that will keep you moving. It's just as inspiring as working on your own stuff... maybe even more inspiring when you get right down to it."

"What is it?"

"Do something for somebody else."

"You mean like charity?"

Granddaddy shrugged. "Yes, that works, but there are lots of things you can do for other people that don't fall under the heading of charity. Do something nice for someone out of the blue. Like when you talked about taking Jenn to a chick flick without her having to ask. The point is to think about what you can do to help someone. Don't think money or charity, think about what someone else might need."

"I don't really know anyone who needs anything... well, I know people who might need things, but they are things I can't help with. I can't help someone get a car."

"Maybe not a car, but you know a lot about working out. Is there anybody you can think of who could use some help with that?"

"Maybe, but why would they listen to me?"

"They might not. It kind of depends on how you offer. It might not work if you walk up to someone and tell them they're doing it all wrong. Just put yourself in their shoes and remember how it felt when you first started out. When you see someone getting something wrong, think of what you would have been okay hearing back when you were making those same mistakes. The best rule of thumb is to remember that it's not *what* you say that matters as much as *how* you say it. Don't talk down to people. Don't be condescending, or rude, or mean."

Granddaddy held up his hands. "I know you won't be any of those things, but sometimes it takes a little practice to figure out how to teach or tell other people things. As long as your goal is always to treat them with the respect and dignity every human being has a right to, you'll do okay."

"What happens if they don't want any help?"

"Then they aren't ready. If that happens, your big challenge will be not taking it personally. If people aren't ready to accept what someone else is offering them, then they aren't ready. There's nothing you can do about that. You can't make someone ready to accept what you have to offer. But as soon as you realize they aren't ready, you'll find your own motivation in full force because you are ready."

Granddaddy turned towards me shaking his head. "I gotta warn you, though. Doing things for other people gets addicting too. There's nothing quite like seeing a genuine smile on someone's face and knowing you played a part in putting it there. It will fill you up. And when you feel like crap, or when you're stuck, or when you can't figure out what to do next, doing something for someone else will start kicking off the cobwebs until you're ready to get back on track. It's the whole GOYA thing. When you can't GOYA for yourself, then GOYA for someone else!"

I smiled. I liked the way that sounded. GOYA... I was definitely going to have to write that down. Maybe even write it in big letters on a single sheet of paper and tape it to my wall. Maybe the inside of my locker too. GOYA... got it!

"Hey. It's stopped raining," Granddaddy said.

I looked out and he was right. The wind had died down and there was blue sky off in the distance.

Granddaddy continued, "I guess we're lucky it stopped raining before you had to take off for work."

I nodded, but I was feeling a little sad.

"If you leave now, you'll have plenty of time to get there in case it starts again."

I stared down at the floor. "Will you be around again? I mean... so we can talk again sometime?"

Granddaddy nodded. "I'll be around. I don't know when we'll talk next, but I've been keeping my eyes and ears on you all these years. That's not going to stop anytime soon. I promise."

I smiled and nodded. "Cool."

"And before I forget," Granddaddy said reaching into his jacket. "Here's something for you."

I looked at what he handed me. It was a leather-bound book, the leather soft and worn. When I opened it, all the pages were blank. I smiled at Granddaddy. "Thanks!"

"Okay!" Granddaddy exclaimed clapping his hands together.

Then he jumped down from the picnic table in one quick motion.

I jumped down too, but not quite as gracefully.

He clapped a hand on my shoulder. "Now, remember what I said when we started talking. I don't expect you to remember everything we talked about today. You'll remember a lot of it, but even the stuff you don't remember is in your mind now, so when you need it, it'll be there for you." Granddaddy looked around. "Okay... time to GOYA!"

I nodded, turned, and started to walk towards work. I took a deep breath and was surprised. The air did smell different than it had before.

"Hey... Dakota!" Granddaddy called out.

I stopped and turned. "Yeah?"

"I'm proud of you. You're a good kid."

I beamed and nodded at him, and then started walking again. I was so full I could barely stand it. Then I realized I hadn't thanked him and I really wanted to. I wanted to shake his hand and say thank you the way he'd shown me.

I turned and started jogging back to the pavilion, but he was gone. I stopped and listened, but couldn't hear anything other than the wind, the leaves, and the birds.

I was totally amazed that he could disappear so quickly and so completely. I knew there had to be a logical explanation, but I couldn't help but wonder if he'd just stepped out of this place and into that other world he goes to when he's not around. I still have no idea where that other place is, but I do feel like he left me with a bunch of clues for getting there.

MY JOURNAL

November 30th

Today was great. My head is still busting with all the stuff Granddaddy said to me. He gave me this book, and I couldn't wait to write in it. I don't want to forget the things he said, so I'm going to write them here. I'll write the name of the first book I read here too. I don't want to forget it like Granddaddy did.

My girlfriend asked... rats! JENN asked me how things went today, but all I could say was that it was great. It's not that I didn't trust her enough to tell her about it. I'm just not sure how to explain it yet. I wanted to write down what I remembered first. Then maybe I'll be able to tell her about it.

Here's what I remember so far:

- Remember people's names. It's a sign of respect.
- Look for people to read about so I can learn more about how to be successful.
- Everybody started out as a teenager, even successful people.
- Keep making plans for your future.
- Find a way to enjoy doing things I don't like to do.
- GOYA... Get Off Your Ass!
- Gratitude... I have to think about this one some more. I know what it is, but I haven't had much experience with

feeling it, so I'm not sure I know what it feels like yet. I know how grateful I am that Granddaddy spent time with me today. Maybe I can use that as a reference point and build from there.

From what Granddaddy said, it sounds like I've been doing a pretty good job on my own. That was nice to hear. It's tough sometimes. At least now I have all the stuff Granddaddy said. I wonder if Colonel Reynolds is still alive. Granddaddy didn't say... but I didn't ask either.

I'm going to the library tomorrow to get my first book. I don't know what it will be yet, but that's okay.

Granddaddy also said he was proud of me. Never heard those words before.

Thanks!

*If you really enjoyed reading this book, please check out its sequel, *A Sprint to the Top: How to win the game of life.*

Peek inside of, *A Sprint to the Top*: https://ti-nyurl.com/yao4azoa

*If you're an educator and would like to learn more about, *The Storm's Student Workbook and Teacher Workbook*,: https://tinyurl.com/vcvxu5h and https://tinyurl.com/y9xyy35a

*Also, book reviews are a huge help to we authors. I promise it's easy to do. Please leave an honest review right here: https://tinyurl.com/ybvm9wlz

*Next, please join my email list so I can share some great offers with you: http://granddaddyssecrets.com/

Granddaddy's Secrets Book Series

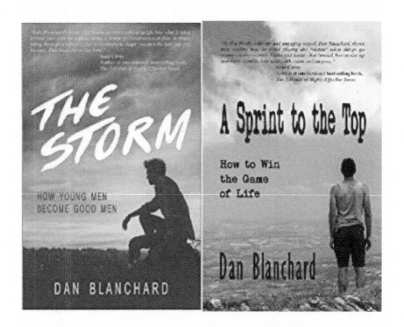

**An amazing story of improving your self-worth
that you'll never forget!**

As still just a teen, can Dakota master his Granddaddy's Secrets before life knocks him down for good? Living a life of hope against a backdrop of despair, violence, and poverty, Dakota's life is broken, and he's trying to fix it the best way he can. He's working hard to live a future better life than the terrible one he's now enduring.

Dakota hates the way he is living. And he so badly wants to break out of his hellhole. Finally, he needs to feel good about himself and this world. But life always seems to be conspiring against Dakota, starting with his own violent and drunk father, followed by his rough neighborhood and school. He knows he must find a better way to live his life, or he'll become the thing that scares him the most, his father. He can't bear the thought of living a life of never-ending struggle, especially while he still thinks that success, happiness, and becoming a good man are within his reach if he acts now.

The Storm and *A Sprint to the* Top are an indispensable books for teens. But so are they for parents, grandparents, teachers, coaches, and anyone else who influences young people or need a reminder themselves how to get back on track. *They are* endorsed by Sean Covey- author of "The 7 Habits of Highly Effective Teens", Rodney Smith- Olympic Bronze medalist wrestler, Tebucky Jones- New England Patriots Super Bowl Champion, Dan Gable- Olympic Gold Medalist and Athlete of the Century, as well as a myriad of other high-achievers. So, don't wait any longer to join these amazing people. Invest in yourself right now by getting this book.

Granddaddy's Secrets for Educators Book Series

Finally, a series that will make educators' lives easy and better!

From Book 1: Are you one of the millions of urban educators out there that wish professional development was more relevant and useful? We, educators, understand how broke our professional development and evaluation system is. We all know that today's educators need better professional development and an effective way to evaluate it. Teachers want to be the best teachers that they can become. Furthermore, they also want all of their students' performance to improve. A good education is the best way for our youth to become capable leaders of tomorrow.

Unfortunately, professional development and a practical way to evaluate it is very complicated. The process of transferring expertise to and through educators and then into students in a meaningful way that increases student performance is very problematic as a long history of subpar student performance in our urban schools has demonstrated. Professional development and evaluation programs must become better if we will have any chance of transferring expertise from the experts to the teachers and then to the students. We have to prepare our urban youth better. If we fail in our mission of better preparing our youth through professionally developing and evaluating our educators, then the mediocre or even subpar performance of our students will continue.

The reading of this book is paramount for college professors and their aspiring educator students and school administrators, department heads, lead teachers, the education field, and the people who serve it in general. Daniel Flores- author, speaker, educator of the year endorses this book. So does many of his peers. So, don't wait any longer to join these amazing educators. Invest in yourself right now by getting this book.

Authors Should Speak Book Series

Finally, a simple, common-sense approach that helps authors sell their books!

From Book 1: Are you one of the many authors who want to sell more books? Today's authors know it is hard to sell books. The traditional way of book sales no longer works as it once did. We authors know we need a better approach now. Today's authors want to get better at selling books and getting their message out there. Authors wish to help the right people at the right time.

Sadly, the lack of exposure is holding us authors back from spreading our message to the people who need our expertise the most. People are bombarded by marketing all day long. This has caused most people to tune out the messages, including our own, to help them. We must learn to effectively speak to the right people at the right time through public and professional speaking. We must better hone our message, what our book is about, and how it helps others through speaking. This would help more people who need our answers and help us authors sell more books as well.

If we authors don't learn to fine-tune our message through speaking, we will continue to have low book sales. Furthermore, we will also have wasted a lot of time writing a book because so few people will know about it. This book is endorsed by international author and TEDx Speaker Jeff Davis and many other authors and speakers worldwide. So, don't wait any longer to join these fantastic people. Invest in yourself right now and sell more books as well by picking up this one.

Granddaddy's Secrets for Sports Lovers Book Series

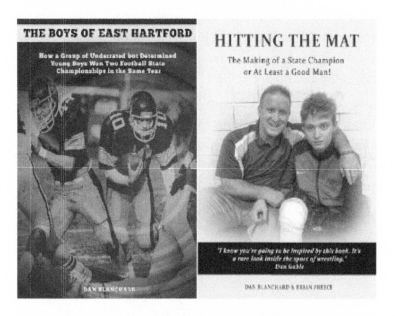

If you enjoy sports, you're really going to enjoy these sports books!

From Book 1: Don't you just love a good coming of age story? The Boys of East Hartford reminds us that growing up is tough sometimes, especially when one comes from the wrong neighborhood or even the wrong side of the state. This group of unassuming boys from East Hartford is trying to give themselves and their community something to believe in again. They want to matter. They desire to be someone special. They have to grow into good men who win big football games. The Boys of

East Hartford want to go out on top their last year of high school.

However, to win the big one, The Boys of East Hartford are going to have to overcome injuries, low morale, and their own coach who psychologically beats them up in the name of making them tougher. They will have to survive mishaps, living, and playing in a northern town rather than the southern powerhouse part of the state. They will have to take on a top-ranked, unbeatable Hamden with their ferocious defense and unstoppable offense stacked with future top-tier college and pro players. The Boys of East Hartford must come together as a team that will have to dig deeper and play football better than anyone thinks is possible. They must stop Hamden's unstoppable offense if they are to have any chance at all of not getting blown out, humiliated, and possibly injured.

If they don't find a way to play better than they've ever played before, they risk going back broken to a lack-luster life in an old factory town that is fading. If they do the unthinkable, they may somehow pull off the biggest upset in Connecticut football history as the new State Champs. This book is endorsed by East Hartford Legend Ernie Hutt of Augie and Rays, East Hartford Gazette owner Bill Doak, Athlete of the Decade, Bobby Stefanik, and a host of other ex-athletes, media personalities, local politicians, and East Hartfordites. So, don't wait any longer to join these amazing people. Invest in yourself right now by getting this touching story guaranteed to remind you of what's possible when everyone believes in the impossible.

Granddaddy's Secrets for Parents Book Series

Finally, an easy-going fun parenting book series to make a parent's life more fun!

From Book 1: Parents, are you tired of being overworked and underappreciated? Do you fear that nothing you do is good enough? Being a parent in today's times is more challenging than ever. Sometimes the world just seems broken. And we parents are doing the best we can to fix what we can by raising good kids. We all desire to be great parents and give our kids extraordinary lives. We all want happy and successful families. Sadly, the trials of life, the lack of time and resources often wear us down, so we aren't always at our best around our children. Society rewards terrible behavior too often, making it harder for our children to understand us when we say no to them. We must remember to have patience with ourselves and our children. In this book, you will learn how to parent them out of love and what great parents do. We must find a better way to raise our kids than what they are seeing in society.

If we fail, our children's well-being and future are at stake here, and so is society's. As great parents, we can have a life of happiness and success for our families or we can live in never-ending drudgery and mishaps if we drop the ball. This book is endorsed by successful parents from all over the world. So, don't wait any longer to join these fantastic people. Invest in yourself, your family, and the future right now by getting this book.

Granddaddy's Secrets for Self-Starters
Book Series

**Become a self-starter and you will become
more successful!**

From Book 1: Are you one of those self-starters determined to
be successful and enjoy the better things in life? If you are, you
already know that the world is not fair and isn't going to hand
you anything. You already know that you have to take charge
of creating the future that you want. And what do you want?
Well, if you're a self-starter, you want to take the initiative to
create more success in your life. You also want to be the one
in charge of your own life and the one who makes things happen that bring you success and happiness, right?

However, none of this will be easy. Life's trials and tribulations always seem to be standing in the way. Sometimes the masses of society are against you. And sometimes, even your own friends and family are holding you back in the name of trying to protect you. You're tired of the lack of momentum and the lack of know-how getting in your way. Now you know you must stay motivated, gain the know-how, and get moving again through this book because you must climb to the top and win the game of life.

If you succeed at being a self-starter, the world opens up where anything is possible. If you stay put and don't start to build the momentum you need, you risk living a subpar existence where you're grinding it out every day and just getting by in life. Don't let the 'start' stop you! This book has been endorsed by a myriad of successful and motivated people who most certainly are self-starters. Are you? If so, don't wait any longer to join this group of winners. Invest in yourself right now by getting this book.

Granddaddy's Secrets for Frustration Beaters Book Series

Finally, a trilogy that will kick your frustrations down the road by turning them into victories right here and right now!

From Book 1: Does life frustrate you? Do you want to know how to overcome that frustration? Hey, we all know the world is a tough place. Heck, sometimes it's even a broken place, right? I bet you don't want to be frustrated and stressed anymore, huh? I know you want to beat back your frustrations and win more often. You want to take charge of your own life and be happy again.

Unfortunately, life's trials, tribulations, and frustrations are standing in the way of your success and happiness. It seems like some secret hidden force is always messing things up for us, doesn't it? Right now, you must overcome your frustration and find a way to win so you won't be frustrated anymore with life. You know, deep down inside, you have to find the secrets to life that will make you a winner and happy again.

If you do nothing, you will continue to be stressed out and frustrated over living a subpar life. Suppose you learn how to overcome your frustrations and move forward. In that case, you can be happy again, celebrating your never-ending successes. This book has been endorsed by many impressive people who were once just like you, frustrated. Don't wait any longer to join this group of frustration beaters who are now reaching for their dreams. Invest in yourself, your future, and your well-being right now by getting this book.

Granddaddy's Secrets for Overachievers
Book Series

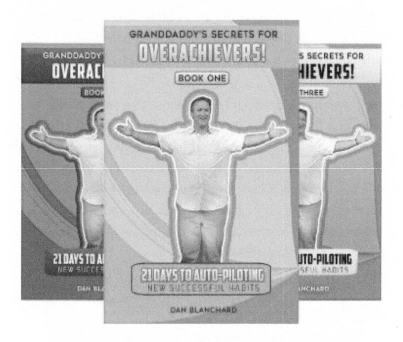

**This book series will help you achieve far more
than you ever thought was possible!**

From Book 1: Are you one of those highly driven overachievers trying to fix the world by being more than average? Would you like to be an overachiever? I know you want to win and be the best you can, don't you? You want to take charge of your own life and be successfully happy, right?

Unfortunately, sometimes life stands in the way of our winning. And so does what we don't know. Sometimes it seems like the universe is secretly conspiring against us not to let us get ahead in this world. Occasionally other people hold us back as well. However, you won't let these trials and tribulations stop you. You want to be the best. And you know that you must find the secrets to success so you can win the game of life.

This book will help you make sure that you're doing everything you can to not fail. You know what is at stake here... an average life of forever being dissatisfied or an extraordinary life of being forever elated. This book is endorsed by some very successful people who know what it means to take charge of their own lives and be those overachievers that others admire. So, don't wait any longer to join this prestigious group. Invest in yourself right now by getting this book.

Granddaddy's Secrets for Authorpreneurs Book Series

At last, a simple series built for indie authors trying to figure out how to push their self-published book closer to being a business that actually earns them money!

From Book 1: Are you one of the millions of authors out there who are not satisfied with the number of books you are selling? As an author, indie author, or self-published author, you are already fully aware of the power of the pen and how your expertise can improve millions' lives. You want that message to get out there via a lot more book sales. You also want to finally take charge of your own life and create the world you want through an author business that you have full control over.

However, the learning curve is very steep for just one person to manage. You may not have the right connections and resources to gain wide exposure to your books. Heck, you may not even have all the know-how yet to make up for those lack of resources. You must learn the tricks of successful authorpreneurs. You must discover your own secrets of success to be the type of author you want to be to help change the world someday. And you must become more resourceful when competing against the big boys who have deep pockets and vast resources.

Writing a book is a huge endeavor. It's something that 85% of the people out there want to do, but only 15% actually accomplish. If you stop now as an author of one book, instead of becoming an authorpreneur of a business based on your books, you may have spent all that time writing your first book for naught. Learn the secrets to authorpreneurship success, and you could sell a ton of books that change the world. Or, don't learn these secrets, and sadly, your sales and impact will be next to nothing. This book has been used and endorsed by successful authors who have taken their book business to the next level. So, don't wait any longer to get on board and join these successful authors. Invest in yourself and your author book business right now by getting this book and learning what it takes to graduate from an author to an authorpreneur.

Free Sample Chapter of the Next Book in this Series:

A Sprint to the Top

1

After The Storm

"I'm not afraid of storms, for I am learning how to sail my ship."

— Louisa May Alcott

When the rain finally stopped, I stepped outside where the smell of the storm had quickly been replaced by the smell of clean fresh rejuvenating air. It was time to start my paper route, but I stopped long enough to take a deep breath and think about the fact that exactly one year ago today, Granddaddy and I had spent the afternoon in the park. My life had changed since the day he shared his secrets for living a great life with me. Before that afternoon, I'd believed I was doing okay. But after we talked, I felt like I was going to bust with all the amazing things he talked about. It had been too much for me to fully grasp in one sitting, but just as Granddaddy had promised, with each passing day more things made sense.

Sometimes remembering the way I used to think before that day makes me laugh. It had been my 16th birthday, and his

76th. Before talking to Granddaddy I actually believed that luck played a bigger role in my accomplishments than I did, and that luck would take over and get the job done when I couldn't. Maybe I thought that way because when it came to sports, people had a tendency to say things to me like "lucky break" when I did something no one expected me to be able to do. Now I understand that you don't need luck on your side to get things to turn out the way you want them to. And that what might look like luck to other people is more likely the result of hard work that's prepared us to take advantage of opportunities when they show up. I'd always been good at the hard work part, but I'd worked even harder over the last year and was feeling more confident than ever—like nothing could ever get in my way again.

I looked towards the early morning horizon and the beautiful rainbow shimmering into existence and smiled as another one of Granddaddy's secrets popped into my mind. He said that we should learn to appreciate life's "storms" because we all have storms in our lives. I'd already lived through a bunch of my own storms and knew there would be more. That was okay though, because storms produced rainbows too. I just needed to keep looking for them.

When I left Granddaddy last year, in that moment, I knew my life was going to be different. With each step I felt bigger, stronger, and more fortunate. When I turned back to thank him again, my mysterious Granddaddy was nowhere to be seen. He'd told me that even though I hadn't seen him, he'd been watching my progress while I was growing up and that he'd been at most of my wrestling matches and football games. He also said there were reasons why I never saw him, and reasons why it had to be that way. He didn't explain the reasons, but I didn't ask either. Considering how quickly he vanished that day, I just reckoned it was one of his many amazing skills.

Now it was a year later, and thanks to Granddaddy, I was more at peace with myself and the world around me. It was a good feeling, but there was something sad in it too because I hadn't seen him other than the few hours we'd spent together last year. What was I going to do if he didn't show up today? Or if I never saw him again? I had no idea. Either way, one thing was true… that day in the park had been one of the best days of my life! Since that day, I've tried my best to practice the secrets Granddaddy shared. For instance, I wasn't going to settle for just thinking I might be successful. I knew without a doubt I could be successful. I was going to live my life, doing all the things I told Granddaddy I would do, and be a success as a result.

When I got up this morning, I started my day the same way I start every day, visualizing my future success as if it were already a done deal. I'd been doing that for almost a year before my afternoon with Granddaddy, and for the most part, things were working out. Last year my wrestling team had a good year. We didn't place in the state championships like I'd visualized, but I placed as an individual. This year's football season just ended, and we did great, falling just one game short of the championship playoffs. Wrestling season was starting this coming Monday and I was already visualizing a successful season for both me and my team, while walking my morning newspaper route.

And even though I was only a junior, I'd already written down my goals for my senior year too: To win the state championships in both football and wrestling, to be the captain of both the football and wrestling teams, and to win the individual state wrestling title at the 145-pound weight class. The great part about knowing what my goals for next year are is that it makes it easier to figure out what I can do right now to set myself up for my future success. And thanks to Granddaddy's encouragement, I've started thinking about my success beyond high school too, which means thinking and planning my success beyond sports. I visualize opening my college acceptance letter and receiving my bachelor's diploma. I added getting better grades to my to-do list too. No more average grades for me! It's things like that that really make me feel like I'm taking charge of my destiny. And, I believe I can make it happen.

Granddaddy was the first person I ever told about how I wrote my goals down and visualized them as if they'd already actually happened. I was worried he would say that I was being too cocky, but he said that confidence was a necessary part of success, because without it, we wouldn't have the courage to reach for anything. "You've got to aim for something, so you might as well shoot for the stars. If you miss with the moon, you'll have accomplished more than most, you'll have a victory to celebrate, and you can still shoot for the stars."

He made me feel good about doing it too. He said that writing down my goals and thinking about them would make a tremendous difference in the long run. He told me to keep doing it, and I gave him my word that I would. We didn't talk about what giving my word meant that day, but it makes sense that if you give your word to someone and then don't keep it, it would be hard for that person, or anyone else, to trust or respect you. I was determined to be a man of my word because I wanted to have a solid reputation as a person who could be depended on to come through with what he said or promised.

Sometimes I wonder how much the way I think about things matters. There's a poster in one of our classrooms with the saying "Everything starts as a dream." It sounds true enough. If people didn't think about how to change things or make them better, we probably wouldn't have cars or computers because those things started out as dreams and ideas. I've heard a couple of famous people say that "thoughts become things" and that kind of makes sense too. If everything starts as a dream, well, a dream is a thought. If you keep thinking about it and how to make it happen, it's more likely to happen. Isn't that what Steve Jobs did with Apple? He had a dream about what a computer should be and didn't stop working on his dream until he was holding it in his hand.

Now when I look around, I don't just see stuff that's cool or useful. I can look at anything and know that it started out as a dream, idea, or thought in someone's head. Like most people, I've just gotten so used to having the things other people's dreams created around me that I wasn't thinking about what I might be able to do with my own dreams, ideas, and thoughts. I'm working on changing that by paying more attention to what I'm thinking about, but there are still plenty of times when my mind still wanders into the weird. At first I tried to figure out where those thoughts came from, but I gave up on that. What difference does knowing where they came from make? I'd rather focus on something I can actually control so that when I realize my thoughts are somewhere in outer space, I can regroup and refocus them in a better direction... because if my thoughts are going to become things, I'm going to do as much as I can to make sure they are good things!

One thing that really helped was figuring out that it's impossible to think two thoughts at the same time. For example, you can't think a negative thought and a positive thought at the same exact time. There isn't enough room for both of them in our brain—well at least not in my brain. At first I thought the goal was to not think any negative thoughts at all, but that was impossible. Instead, I got better at noticing when my thoughts were negative. When they were, I'd come up with something positive to think about instead. As soon as I shifted my focus onto a better thought, it pushed the negative thought right out of my mind.

I've been working on this for about six months now, and during that time I haven't come across one negative thought worth thinking about. They all lead to the same result too—living a life decided by someone else. I distinctly remember Granddaddy talking about the difference between living a life that's the result of the choices we deliberately make, and the default life society is always ready to provide when we accept the choices and decisions others are happy to make for us. As far as I'm concerned, there is only room for positivity in my brain because I'm going to live a life I chose.

It's like putting together links in a chain. I start by thinking about what I want. Then I figure out steps I can take to get me there. The steps are important because if I don't do anything, I'm not going anywhere no matter how much I want to. Pretty soon, the things I'm thinking and doing are all headed in the same direction. That means that if I think about something positive long enough, I'll eventually start acting in a way that's consistent with getting that positive thing. So I work hard on keeping my thoughts, actions, and behaviors in line with my goals, and am getting better at making decisions about which kinds of actions and behaviors will lead me to the future I want.

Over the past week I'd visualized meeting up with Grand-daddy today about a million times. There were so many things I wanted to tell him about—like about all the reading I'd done since last November. At first I didn't think I was going to like it much, but this kind of reading was different. It wasn't like it was in school when I had to read about what happened to some-one, or about what someone did. I was reading about real peo-ple, and about what really happened to them and around them. Most of them are long gone, but that didn't change the fact that at one time they were living, breathing and walking around just like I was right now.

Last week I read something General Patton of WWII said. "Fear kills more people than death. Death only kills once." If I hadn't spent that time in the park with Granddaddy, chances are very slim that I would have picked up that book and started reading it. But we did have our day in the park, and every day since, something I learned from him encourages me to think. That day in the park changed my life forever and I do my best to stay true to the lessons he shared. I thank God for that day, and for my Granddaddy.

ABOUT THE AUTHOR

Dan Blanchard is a bestselling and award-winning author, speaker, educator, TV Host, two-time junior Olympian wrestler, two-time junior Olympian wrestling coach, and a double veteran of our U.S. military. He has successfully completed fourteen years of college, earned seven degrees, and teaches in Connecticut's largest inner-city high school.

He believes it is our duty to positively inspire and guide our youth every chance we get. As he says, *"It isn't fair to expect kids to know how to become citizens and leaders without help. It's up to us to help them."*

Dan has been employing this philosophy throughout his 20-plus years as a teacher and coach. After repeatedly being asked by his students to write a book so other teens could hear what he was saying, he was inspired to sit down and write *The Storm?*

In addition, Dan has been a featured guest on both radio and television, is one of the ten people January Jones wrote about in her newest book *Priceless Personalities*, is one of the experts featured in parenting expert Bill Corbett's book: *The Expert's Guide to Teenagers,* is a Teacher Consultant for the University of Connecticut's Writing Project, and was chosen by the American Federation of Teachers of Connecticut as their face and voice of education reform.

You can contact Dan through his website at www.Granddaddys Secrets.com

***Please follow Dan on Amazon:** http://www.amazon.com/-/e/B00KEO611E*

Made in United States
North Haven, CT
07 September 2022